CAPE MAY MONARCH BUTTERFLIES

CLAUDIA VANCE

CHAPTER ONE

"This is much too stressful," Liz said as she frantically ran around the Seahorse Inn trying to get it ready for the monarch butterfly group that was set to arrive the following day.

Margaret sighed. "I can't believe Dolly and Kim forgot to tell us about this two-week group booking. I'm not exactly feeling prepared, and I don't know a thing about these monarch butterflies except that they're orange and black, quite beautiful, and stop here during their migration south."

Liz grabbed some groceries from one of the paper bags sitting on the kitchen counter that they'd just brought in. "Well, I guess we're just going have to figure this out. They're coming from Pittsburgh, you said?"

Margaret nodded as she grabbed fruit out of another grocery bag and placed it into some bowls on the island. "Yeah, I believe it's a garden club from Pittsburgh, and they're driving a long way to come here. I think some may even be flying in."

Just then, Irene, Jackie, and Bonnie, their new hires at the B&B, entered the kitchen. "What can we do to help you two?" Irene asked.

Liz pulled out a pack of butterfly napkins and set them on

the counter. "Well, this is the only butterfly related item I could find at the store, some napkins. Can you think of anything else we can incorporate to make this a little more butterfly themed at the Seahorse? We're grasping at straws here."

Jackie scrunched her brow and scratched her head when a light bulb went off. "Why don't we go out and find some monarch butterfly themed items. Maybe we can add a few touches here and there around the B&B. Nothing crazy."

Bonnie clapped her hands and went to the foyer to grab her purse in the closet. "That sounds perfect. I'll go start the car."

Irene shrugged her shoulders then looked at Liz and Margaret as Bonnie and Jackie ran out to the car. "Is that OK with you two? They didn't even wait for a response."

Margaret smiled and chuckled, while walking to her purse. "We will take any help we can get to make this experience great for our guests. I'll give you my card to go grab some things."

Irene took Margaret's card, smiled and waved goodbye, then she walked out the door to meet Bonnie and Jackie at the car.

Liz threw her hair up in a bun and let out the loudest groan Margaret had ever heard. "I don't know, Margaret. I sure hope our guests have their own monarch butterfly experiences booked, because I don't know what we're going to do with them. I'm not sure what Dolly meant by telling the group we would provide monarch activities."

Margaret placed a few of the butterfly napkins on the hutch in the lobby neatly next to some tea cups, then stood back to admire her work. "Well, I'm sure they have some things booked. I don't think they're relying on a bed-and-breakfast to provide all of their activities for the time they are here."

An hour or so had gone by before Irene, Jackie, and Bonnie

loudly walked through the front door with stuffed bags from their shopping trip.

Margaret and Liz's eyes widened in disbelief. "What exactly did you all buy while you were out? The entire store?" Liz asked.

Irene laughed nervously. "Well, it turns out a little store we found had all kinds of butterfly themed items on discount. We may have gone a little overboard, but I think it's going to be fabulous."

Jackie nodded as she pulled a handcrafted delicate orange and black monarch butterfly garland from her large paper shopping bag. "Just look at this gorgeous garland. I am too excited to decorate this place."

Bonnie pulled a butterfly cake mold out of her bag. "And this will be perfect for the cake I'm going to make for teatime."

Margaret pondered asking how much money they had spent on these unnecessary items, but then she thought better of it. They hadn't really decorated the B&B in months and it was kind of nice to see it all festive again, even if it wasn't for a holiday but rather a special occasion in Cape May.

Liz immediately helped Irene, Jackie, and Bonnie unpack their bags of goodies while gawking at some of the ornate items they had found. "Well, we at least have the decor down, but we don't know too much about monarch butterflies, do we?"

All the women looked at each other, shook their heads, and shrugged. How had they lived in Cape May for so long without any knowledge of the fascinating species that was closely linked with their town?

Margaret thought for moment. "You know, there's a little place that might have some useful information. You all decorate, and I'll try and find some educational materials for us."

Margaret grabbed her purse and stepped outside. Greeted by a warm but slightly chilly late-September breeze coming from the ocean right across the street, she held her keys in

3

hand and walked to her car with purpose. She knew where she was going. It was a little hidden place that she hadn't been to in years, but she had a feeling that they might have exactly what she was looking for.

After a five-minute drive, Margaret parked the car down a narrow alley and walked a hidden path to a little old store that was known to locals. From the outside, it looked exactly the same as it had the last time she'd been there many years ago. She paused and admired the beautiful fall foliage that had started to turn shades of red, yellow, and orange all around her and the many pumpkins and gourds that lined the little cobblestone path to the shop.

She opened the rickety door slowly, and a small bell chimed. Walking inside, the smell of old books and the sound of Ella Fitzgerald overwhelmed her senses. A fat black cat was nestled in the window between a display of autumn books. It meowed and stretched, then rolled over to a different sleeping position, seemingly unfazed by the new visitor. Greeting customers was apparently not in its job description. There were only two other people in the store, and they were in the back room discussing cookbooks.

An older gentleman—in his eighties and sporting bifocals —appeared from behind a curtain covering the backroom doorway. He made his way slowly to the register. "Can I help you?" the man asked.

Margaret was still in her element, taking in the smells, sights, and sounds of the unique little bookshop hidden away in their lovely town. Since it'd been so long since she'd been there, a lot of nostalgia rushed back and hit her all at once. She used to come here with her dad when she was in high school. He loved going to the bookshop to look for novels and comic books while she would usually end up in the young adult section, picking out her mysteries and thrillers that she used to love so much. It was their time together when Liz was busy with her school activities and her mother was late getting home from work. They didn't get much one-on-one time together, but when they did, it was at this bookshop and for that it held a special place in her heart.

Margaret held her hand on her heart and looked over at the man. "Well, hi it's nice to see you. I haven't been here in over twenty years, and I'm pretty sure you were here then."

The man coughed then let out a loud laugh. "Yep, I'm the owner, and I haven't retired to the dismay of my wife and children. I love it too much, and frankly, retirement is for old people. Working keeps me young, and I love being here. What can I help you with today?"

Margaret looked up at a history book of Cape May, pulled it down and started flipping through the pages. "Well, I'm actually here looking for a book about the monarch butterflies. I need to quickly educate myself about them and what they do here in Cape May. We have some visitors at our B&B coming specifically to see them. I know I could go on the internet, but I'd really like something tangible. Something I can keep for the guests to pick up and read."

The man shifted his eyes for a minute, then held his finger in the air as though a light bulb had turned on in his mind. "It's funny you should say that, I just had a gentleman drop off a ton of old butterfly books. Follow me."

Margaret's eyes lit up. She felt like she was on a hunt for some kind of treasure to unlock the secrets of the butterflies. She followed him to the back room, where she noticed that the ceilings became a lot higher, almost like a vaulted church ceiling. How had she not remembered this? There was a rolling ladder amongst the very tall shelves stuffed with books, which the man grabbed and started walking up, but not before Margaret stopped him.

"Let me do that. I don't want to force you to go up this ladder," Margaret said.

The man looked at Margaret with a little skepticism and also a little concern but then ultimately decided to let her go up. "Be careful, please. Go halfway up the ladder, and on your right, you'll see about fifteen different books that should have information on monarch butterflies somewhere in them."

The cat that had been napping in the window appeared in the back room and walked straight up to the man, sat at his feet, and looked up at him while meowing loudly. The man chuckled and looked down at the cat. "Sampson, I know it's breakfast time. Can you give me a minute?"

The cat let out a little chirp and started furiously purring, still staring at him all the while.

The man sighed. "OK, fine. Let's go get your wet food and kibble. I'll be right back to make sure you find what you need, ma'am. By the way what's your name?"

Margaret stretched off the ladder as she grabbed a book then opened it with one hand and looked down at him. "Oh, I'm Margaret, and what's your name? I haven't been here in so long, but I feel as though I should know it."

"I'm Richard. It's nice to meet you. You know, I have a daughter around your age. All right, well, I'll be right back."

Margaret stood on the ladder, flipping through the book pages, looking at all the beautiful photographs of butterflies and insects, and felt so at peace and happy—a stark difference to how she'd felt a little bit ago at the B&B. Then, she'd been full of anxiety and stress over hosting the guests who were arriving tomorrow. She grabbed the rest of the books from the shelf, hugged them into her chest with one arm, then carefully stepped down the ladder. Before she reached the bottom, she spotted a small red velvet lounge chair in the corner. Next to the chair was a little end table full of potted spider plants and miscellaneous old wood-carved knickknacks of fisherman in yellow rain jackets. She sat down in the chair, placed her stack of books on the table, propped her feet up on a nearby ottoman, and took a deep sigh as she grabbed the top book and flipped through the pages. She planned on purchasing some of the books, but right now, she simply wanted to bury her head in them. She couldn't wait to learn about these fascinating insects. There was something intriguing about learning something new and having quiet time to herself on an incredibly hectic day.

* * *

Sarah had reopened the coffeehouse that morning after having been closed for the past two weeks while she and Chris were in Costa Rica. Her new hires were essentially training on the job, making it a chaotic scene as Sarah and the staff, both new and old, took on the morning rush of people eager to get their coffee.

While Sarah was training on the register, a woman approached and slammed a fistful of pennies, nickels, and dimes on the counter. "Count it out. That's five dollars. I'll have a large latte, please."

Sarah's eyes widened as she gathered the change in her hand to add up while Dawn, one of her new hires, went to make the latte.

"Oh, Dawn. Hold on, I need to show you how to do that. There's some quirks to that machine," Sarah said as she dumped the rest of the change into the register.

The woman rolled her eyes and scowled. "Are you kidding me? Now I have to wait for you to show her how to make it? I don't even really *like* the coffee here, it's just the only kind I can stomach around this area."

Sarah took a deep breath. The day was not going as planned at all. "Ma'am, your latte will be right up," Sarah said, forgoing Dawn's training in that moment.

Once she finished making the drink, the woman snatched her latte from Sarah's hands, and stormed out the door, dropping a few more pennies from her purse in the process. Before Sarah had a moment to turn and talk to Dawn, a man appeared at the counter.

"I've been waiting two weeks for your amazing croissant. Literally thinking about it the entire time. Can I have two, please?" the man asked, eyeing up the pastry case.

Sarah looked in the case, not seeing the croissants. "We're all sold out, sir. I'm so sorry. Our supplier will have a lot more for us tomorrow if you want to come back then. For now, maybe a muffin instead?"

The man grabbed his head, as if trying to stop himself from having a full-on meltdown. "You're kidding?! How could you have possibly sold out already?"

Sarah sighed, feeling (for not the first time) like she'd gotten into the wrong business. "I'm sorry, sir."

The man, looking completely defeated, walked out of the store, and once outside, he threw his hands up in the air as though he'd had enough for the day.

By then, the line had died down, giving the staff a moment to breathe. Sarah turned to Dawn as she stood next to the register with her. "I want you to know that the way today is going is not the norm around here. Usually, our customers are nothing but respectful and polite. I hope this doesn't scare you off."

Dawn chuckled. "Oh, I've put up with way worse from my kids. I'll be fine."

Sarah breathed a sigh of relief. "Good. I'm glad to hear that. Now let me show you the quirks with our espresso machine."

Dawn followed Sarah over to the machine and was watching her explain when someone sitting in the corner of the coffeehouse caught her eye. "Have you noticed that woman over there? She's been sitting there with a laptop since we opened hours ago."

Sarah glanced over at her, then turned back to Dawn. "Oh, that's common here. A lot of people will bring their laptops and work while drinking coffee."

Dawn scratched her head. "Oh, I knew that. I used to be

one of them. She just seems different. She keeps watching everything the customers and staff do. It's almost like she's taking notes."

Sarah shifted her eyes, then turned to glance back at the woman. This time the woman looked straight at Sarah, crinkled her nose, and abruptly packed up her bags and walked out of the coffeehouse, dumping her full to-go cup in the trash can on the way out.

Dawn shrugged. "Well, that was odd. Why did she just all of sudden leave like that? Did she see us watching her? I wasn't trying to bother her."

Sarah shook her head. "I have no idea," she said as her cell phone rang from her pocket. Sarah turned to Dawn. "Can you man the register for a moment? I have to take this."

Dawn happily obliged while Sarah walked to the back room that was only for employees.

"Hey, Margaret. What's going on?"

Margaret sounded a bit winded as she walked back to her car with a bag full of books. "Hey. I don't know why I didn't think to ask you since I know you sell books at the coffeehouse, but do you have any books on monarch butterflies I could purchase?"

Sarah thought for a moment, then sighed. "You know, you'd think I would, being that my coffeehouse is called Monarch Coffeehouse, but I don't. It's mainly newer fiction books, but you just gave me an idea. Why do you ask?"

Margaret threw her bag into the car as she held her cell phone. "Oh, well I'm trying to learn as much as I can about them before our guests arrive tomorrow. Not to mention, I wanted to have them for our Cape May Visitors to read from. I just bought a bunch at the old used bookstore."

Sarah's eyes lit up. "Oh, at The Book Nook? I used to love going there as a kid. They're still open? I should stop in sometime."

Margaret got into the driver's seat and shut the door

behind her. "They are, and the owner still works there, bless his heart. He's got to be in his eighties by now. He says he doesn't want to retire."

Sarah chuckled while watching Dawn ring up some customers. "Well, thank you for calling. It gave my brain a nice break from the chaos that is happening at the coffeehouse today. I don't know what I was thinking when I decided to reopen after two weeks *and* train my new hires on the same day."

Margaret gasped and held her hand to her mouth. "Oh, no. I hope it gets better for you."

Sarah sighed. "It will, hopefully. I'll give you call later. Maybe you can teach me a thing or two about the monarch butterflies that I don't know already."

CHAPTER TWO

The next morning, Margaret dropped the girls off at school and picked up Liz so they could head to the B&B together. They'd stayed late the day prior cleaning, organizing, and preparing for the large group renting out the Seahorse Inn for two weeks.

As they arrived to the B&B, it was impossible not to notice all of the new outside decorations. Liz stepped out of the car, her eyes twinkling at the dazzling trappings before her going up the steps and strung along the large front porch. "What in the world? This looks amazing, but how did it get here? It wasn't there last night?" Liz admired the butterfly lanterns hanging in place of the usual ferns around the porch.

Margaret lowered her sunglasses as she followed behind Liz, eyeing the colorful purple potted mums with delicate tiny fake orange monarch butterflies clipped on them. "This is gorgeous. Didn't Irene, Bonnie, and Jackie leave with us last night, though?"

Liz nodded as she opened the front door to a monarch butterfly wonderland in the foyer. Margaret stood behind her as they both held their hands to their mouths in astonishment. Before them, spanning the entirety of the foyer, going up the banister, and in the living room, were decorations from floor to ceiling. There were silk pink flowering milkweed stalks and vibrant goldenrod in glass vases, elegant butterfly garlands swagged down the banister, along the hutch, and under the mantel in the living room. There were even more little clip-on monarch butterflies attached to the drapes and other little spots around the room.

Irene appeared at the top of the steps and walked down with a big smile. "What do you two think?"

Margaret walked over to an end table in the foyer, picked up a pair of vintage binoculars, and peered through them. "This is a really nice surprise. You all did a fantastic job."

Irene nodded, feeling proud of herself. "Those binoculars work pretty well, too."

Liz ran her finger alongside a handmade boiled wool butterfly garland hanging above her head. "When did you do all of this? It's stunning. Maybe I should hire you to help me with my interior decorating business," Liz said, half joking.

Jackie walked into the foyer from the kitchen, overhearing the conversation in the process. "Oh, we got here pretty early. We were all very eager and excited to decorate. This was so much fun to do."

Bonnie walked in beside Jackie, propping her arm on Jackie's shoulder. "Yeah, we didn't have time to finish yesterday, so we decided to get here early to ensure it's perfect for the guests when they arrive today. Speaking of which, what time are they expected again?"

Margaret quickly looked at her watch. "They said they'd be arriving around one o'clock. So, we have a few more hours, but I have to say, that I'm feeling less stressed already."

Moments later, a knock came at the door. Everyone stood looking at each other in confusion.

Margaret shrugged. "I'll get it. It's probably just one of the neighbors saying hello." As Margaret opened the door, there stood a large group of people. "Oh, hi there," Margaret said, feeling confused.

"This is the Seahorse Inn, correct?" the woman in the front asked as she stepped back to look at a small name plate sign beside the door.

Margaret nodded. "It is indeed. Are you the group from Pittsburgh?"

The woman nodded. "That would be us, we're the gardening club from Pittsburgh. Can we come in?"

Margaret laughed. "Oh, of course. I'm sorry. I thought that you all weren't arriving until one o'clock."

The Pittsburgh visitors pushed in through the door, most of them in full conversation with one another, pulling their rolling luggage behind them, barely noticing the eye-catching decor.

The woman in the front, who appeared to be the most outspoken of the group, pulled Margaret aside. "Oh, one thing. One couple isn't here yet. They should be arriving sometime tomorrow."

Margaret nodded. "Perfect, well I'm Margaret. My sister, Liz, and I own this B&B. Over there is Irene, Jackie, and Bonnie."

Jackie and Irene grabbed some pieces of luggage. "Let us show you to your rooms so you can get situated," Irene said as she started up the steps with the group following behind.

Once the guests were up the steps and finding their rooms, Liz and Margaret walked into the kitchen together. Liz slumped over the island, propping her head in her hands. "This day has been full of surprises already. I wonder what else is coming."

Bonnie breezed into the kitchen, pulled a hot pie out of the oven, and chuckled. "This reminds me of our days running an inn. I tell you, there was never a boring day."

Margaret smiled. "Well, we are so glad the three of you are here to help us, and that pie smells amazing. What is it?"

Bonnie wiped her hands on her apron. "Oh, it's a peach

slab pie. Perfect served hot with some vanilla ice cream. Would you two like a bite to see how it is?"

Margaret and Liz nodded eagerly, grabbed a couple small plates and forks, and scooped some bites of the delicious tart pie into their mouths.

Margaret shook her head while swallowing. "Bonnie, oh, Bonnie. You are a magician. This is exquisite."

Bonnie blushed and smiled. "I'm glad you like it. Our guests at our old B&B loved it. I'm sure they will here too."

Just then, the outspoken woman from the group arrived in the kitchen with a few others. "I'm sorry, I haven't properly introduced myself. I'm Marcy. This is my husband, Ed. I think that long drive had our brains a little foggy when we arrived, and we forgot our manners."

The couple standing next to Marcy and Ed each extended their hand. The woman said, "We are Susan and Albert, and next to us is Joyce and Brian."

Liz smiled. "Well, it's nice to meet you all. We hear you're here to see the monarch butterflies, is that right?"

Marcy nodded and smiled. "Indeed, we are. We heard all about how they stop over in Cape May during their migration south, and our garden club had the great idea of putting together this trip."

Susan chimed in. "And I'm the one who called the Seahorse and found out you even offer some monarch butterfly excursions. None of the other B&Bs I called offered that, so we *had* to book our stay here."

Joyce looked up at all of the decorations and smiled. "It seems we chose the right place. I'm loving the butterfly theme."

Margaret felt anxiety creep up again and coughed. "Butterfly excursions, you say? You must have spoken to Dolly. What exactly did she tell you about what we offer?"

Susan thought for a moment then pulled out a little notebook in her purse and flipped the pages until she came to a spot with her notes. "Well, she basically said that the B&B would take us to places to see the butterflies."

Liz scratched her head. "Really? Well, I'm sure your group also booked some of your own tours as well? You know to fill in the gaps?"

Susan looked at her notes again, confused. "No. No, we didn't. We assumed the tours were all-inclusive. Is something wrong? Are you not offering the excursions anymore?"

Margaret and Liz looked around the room at the concern now all over the group members' faces.

Margaret scrambled to think of something. "Don't worry about a thing. You'll see the monarch butterflies. We were just ... checking to see if you had booked anything else."

Marcy held her hand over her heart in relief. "Oh, good. You had me a little worried there."

"How's everything going?" Irene asked, walking into the room with Jackie.

Margaret's eyes widened. "Oh, going good. I need to go get some work done in the basement. Irene, if you'd tell the group about Cape May and where to eat, shop, and all of that, that'd be wonderful."

Irene clapped her hands. "Perfect! Well, right next door is a fine restaurant ...."

Margaret grabbed her laptop and motioned to Liz to follow her into the basement theater area.

Once down there, Margaret sat on a recliner and opened her laptop. "Liz, they haven't booked a single thing. Not a *single* thing. What did Dolly get us into? I'm beyond stressed out right now. I have to plan these tours myself."

Liz sat next to her and peered over her shoulder as Margaret feverishly typed things in the search bar. "This is a large group. Will we have to pay out of pocket for these activities? Did they assume it was covered with the price of the room? I hope not. We will be in the negative, if so."

Margaret slammed her laptop shut and picked up her

phone. "I'm calling Dolly to find out. I'm hoping she was smart enough to not say that it was included. She should've known better."

The phone rang and Dolly picked up a little nervously, knowing the guests from Pittsburgh were arriving that day. "Hi, Margaret. How's it going?"

Margaret sighed. "Hi, Dolly. Oh, it's going. The gardening club has assumed we're providing all of their butterfly sight-seeing tours, and they haven't booked even one elsewhere. We are scrambling."

Dolly shook her head. "I think there was some miscommunication there. I said we would provide *an* excursion—as in *one*."

Margaret sighed again. "Really? By the way they're talking, it appears they think it's multiple, or even daily, trips to see the butterflies."

Dolly sighed. "I'm so sorry about all of this, Margaret. Look, why don't Kim and I come back early? I'm sure we can all figure it out together. I don't want you losing money over this."

Liz looked at Margaret, overhearing the conversation. "What do we do? Should they come back?"

Margaret thought for a moment, then shook her head. "No, it's fine. Cape May has some butterfly activities. I'll look some up and book them. I'll explain that the room costs only included one activity and that the rest are out of pocket and that there must have been a mix-up when they booked."

Dolly bit her lip. "That very well may work."

Margaret said goodbye, opened her laptop back up, and typed as fast as she could to find any local butterfly tours. A handful came up, and she clicked availability for tickets on all of them.

Liz looked at the screen as Margaret tried to book tickets. "They're all booked. Every one of them. This isn't going to work at all."

Margaret's heart raced, and she shut her laptop. "We need to figure something else out."

* * *

Across town, Donna prepared for her "first" date with Dale. After their breakup, it was decided that they would start from scratch again, and thus, a new first date would have to happen.

Donna stepped out of the house and got into the car, glancing in the mirror at herself before putting the car into drive and heading to pick up Dale. He still hadn't moved to Cape May, but he did have a little rental property in town to help with the drive between his jobs.

Donna pulled up to Dale's place, and he happily walked outside to meet her, stopping to talk through the car's open window before getting in. "Hey, there. First date, eh? Where are we headed?"

Donna pointed to her cargo pants and vented button-down hiking shirt. "We're going to do a little trail walking, and then maybe grab some dinner. What do you think?"

Dale looked down at the boat shoes he was wearing without socks and his nice silk shirt. "Oh, well, I'm not exactly dressed for it …."

Donna flicked her hand. "You look great, plus it's just a little trail walk. I don't think we'll work up much of sweat or get dirty. Just get in."

Dale shrugged and got in the car. Donna drove to a heavily wooded area twenty-five minutes away, pulling into a sandy parking lot that held only one other car.

"Well, we're here … I think. I found this secret hidden gem online today," Donna said while squinting ahead at the people walking back to their car from the trail.

Dale shifted his eyes. "So, you've never gone here before? Are you sure I'm dressed OK for this?"

Donna looked online at her phone. "Yeah, we're fine. It'll

only be a thirty-minute walk, and then we can get back to the car to go to our dinner reservation."

Dale nodded and proceeded to get out and walk over to the trailhead, looking at a map hung next to it. "Well, it looks like we need to follow the red blazes, and it'll take us in a circle. Seems simple enough."

Donna nodded and started on the path with Dale walking next to her. "It's so serene and quiet. I guess we have the place to ourselves since the only other people parked here left."

Dale brushed his arm against Donna's, and butterflies danced in his stomach. "Look at these monstrous pines. I love it out here."

After a little walking, Dale looked at his watch. "Well, it's been forty minutes. Don't we have to get back to the car?"

Donna scratched her head. "Yeah, we do. The dinner reservation is in thirty minutes. I thought we would've been back by now."

Dale looked at a tree off in the distance. "That's a blue blaze on the tree there. Weren't we following the red blazes? How did we end up on the blue trail?"

Donna shrugged. "I have no idea. Let me grab my phone so we can figure out a way back through my GPS."

Dale did the same and took out his phone. "My phone doesn't have a lick of service. Does yours?"

Donna shook her head. "Nope. Maybe if we walk a little further that way, we'll get some service."

Another ten minutes of walking, and neither of them had service.

Dale looked down at his shirt that had huge sweat stains all over it. "Well, I'm not exactly dressed for dinner anymore."

Donna looked at him and laughed. "I'm so sorry, Dale. I had this whole first date planned out so well. I don't know what happened."

Dale grabbed her hand and kissed it. "Hey, now we're even for that first date I took you on."

Donna laughed. "Oh, you mean the one you took *lots* of girls on."

Dale shook his head in embarrassment. "Don't remind me."

Weather alert signals shrieked from both their phones, interrupting the stillness surrounding them. *Hurricanes coming up the coast now expected to hit NJ in three days.*

Dale looked at the alert. "Well, I guess we have some service now. There's a hurricane coming. Great. I hope this one doesn't clobber the shore towns like that last one years ago. People are still rebuilding."

Donna looked at her phone. "That would be a nightmare. Though, I just got another notification that there is a severe storm warning for our location. We need to book it quick. My GPS says we have to head north to the parking lot, so I think we should turn left by that tree."

Dale put his phone safely back in his pocket and followed Donna down the trail.

After ten minutes of walking, and finally getting back on the red blazed path, the skies went from light gray to dark gray and opened up suddenly. Rain poured down onto them as they went from a fast walk to a full-out run back to the parking lot.

Donna got to the car first, unlocking the doors with her key fob. They both hopped in as the rain pounded the earth all around them.

Dale looked over at Donna, soaking wet from head to toe just like he was, and laughed. "I'm guessing dinner reservations need to be canceled?"

Donna looked at Dale's ruined silk shirt and started cracking up. "I think we need a redo of our redo first date. This did not go as planned."

Dale laughed as they sat in the parking lot watching hard sheets of rain hit the windshield. "How about I get to plan the next one? We'll do this until we get it right."

Donna grabbed Dale's hand, turned the radio on, and

looked out at the rain. "Well, I can't see a thing so we might as well sit here and enjoy the music while watching it. I look forward to what you come up with for the next date."

Dale squeezed her hand and smiled. "This may have been a disaster, but it sure was fun to get caught in a rainstorm with the lady you have a thing for."

CHAPTER THREE

The following day, Margaret decided to take the gardening club out in the morning to possibly see butterflies at a local beach. She'd read somewhere that there were monarch butterfly cluster sightings there. Jackie, Irene, and Margaret each drove a carful of group members and made their way to a little parking area next to Higbee Beach before stepping out of the cars to a cloudy, overcast, drab sky. The air was a little misty, which made it refreshing to be outside. It was pretty quiet out except for another nearby group that was huddled around the dunes, off about a hundred feet ahead. Since Margaret was unsure of where to find monarch butterflies, she ultimately decided to head towards them.

As they began to walk, Bonnie pulled into the parking lot with the last couple to arrive at the Seahorse, having come in a day late.

Stepping out of the car, a woman glanced over at Margaret and the gardening club. "We're here! Don't start without us. Dipsey and Doodle can't wait to walk on the beach."

A very stylish couple exited Bonnie's car, dressed head to toe in designer outfits. The woman wore very high heels and held two yapping teacup Yorkies, Dipsey and Doodle, in her arms. The man wore designer leather loafers, a tie, and a fedora while a gigantic camera with a telephoto lens and large camera flash hung from around his neck. He helped his wife walk unsteadily onto the beach towards where the group had gathered.

Margaret waved to the couple as if to show them where to walk to. "Why are these people dressed for a night out on the town?" she muttered under her breath.

The woman clasped onto her husband's arm for dear life as she tried to stand in the sand without collapsing. "Hi, we're Sharon and Ted. So sorry we're late. I know everyone arrived yesterday. We had something come up," Sharon said as she shushed the barking pups in her arms.

The rest of the group groaned and rolled their eyes on the inside, but politely said their hellos and welcomed the new garden club members to Cape May. Sharon and Ted were very different from everyone else in the group. They were involved with the Pittsburgh club but didn't do any actual gardening themselves. Instead, they paid landscapers to do it all. They were extremely rich and found themselves joining the garden club as an activity during retirement. Though they loved gardens, they didn't actually love touching the dirt or anything involving literal gardening.

"Hi, Sharon and Ted. Welcome! We're attempting to get our first glimpse of the monarch butterflies. I'm Margaret, and over there is Irene and Jackie. You already met Bonnie on the way over," Margaret said as she pointed to everyone.

Ted held his camera up to his eye to look through the lens. "Well, it's nice to meet everyone. Thanks for waiting for us. We're excited to see these butterflies."

Margaret chuckled on the inside since they hadn't been exactly waiting for them—no one had even been sure when they were arriving.

From her pocket, Margaret's phone dinged with a text message from Dave.

Hey, Margaret. You know this hurricane that we keep hearing about out in the Atlantic? My weather guy is saying he thinks it's coming for Cape May, but he's not 100% certain yet. He's saying it should land in a couple days, but I'm going to start boarding up my house. You might need to do the same with the Seahorse, being right across from the ocean. I think your house will be fine since it's more inland. I'll call you later.

Margaret stared at her phone. "A hurricane? Have I been living under a rock? I haven't heard a thing about it. I must have been too busy preparing the bed-and-breakfast. Has anyone heard anything about a hurricane?" she said aloud.

Ted piped in. "Actually, we did hear something about it on our drive here, but the meteorologist seemed to think it would bypass this area."

Marcy's eyes widened. "A hurricane? You're kidding. Last we heard, it was going out to the Atlantic Ocean and was maybe going to clip the northeast area of New Jersey. We wouldn't have traveled here if a hurricane was coming."

Albert flicked his hand in the air. "I'm sure it will pass right over us. I wouldn't worry about it. Let's head over to where those other people are. I think I see some butterflies."

Margaret trailed behind the Pittsburgh group as they made their way across the beach while texting Liz about the hurricane to keep her in the loop.

As they approached the area where the other cluster of people stood, everyone took notice of how quiet they were. They were practically whispering to one another while watching a handful of monarch butterflies near the dunes. Just as the Seahorse guests were close enough to see the butterflies themselves, Dipsey and Doodle started yapping like crazy, then Ted began to snap away with his camera, his flash blinding everyone in the process. The commotion sent the butterflies flying off, and the other group turned around to glare at the Pittsburghers.

A couple in the other group folded their arms and stared at Sharon and Ted. "The noise and that flash chased those butterflies off that we were quietly watching. You have to have some etiquette out here. If you're going to observe nature, you need to make it seem as though you aren't even there," the woman said as they all walked away from their spot.

Ted nervously laughed before putting down his camera. "We apologize. I'm sure we can find some more butterflies around here?"

Margaret looked up and down the beach, not really seeing much. "Well, we can walk along the dunes to see what we can find."

But after about thirty minutes of walking along the dunes, nobody saw much of anything except sand.

Marcy sighed. "Maybe we should find where that other group went? They seem to know how to find the butterflies."

Margaret's eyes widened. She didn't want to bother those people any more than they already had. She looked at the sky again, and felt some worry after thinking about Dave's text. She sensed in her bones that something wasn't right. There was a certain chill to the air that wasn't there yesterday. There was also a stillness and quiet that she wasn't used to.

Irene waved her hand in front of Margaret's face. "Earth to Margaret. You there? Everything OK? You look dazed."

Margaret snapped out of her stupor. "Oh, I was just thinking … You know, today will be a good day to explore the shops and restaurants around Cape May. The butterflies seem to be in hiding, not to mention these skies are looking quite ominous."

* * *

Across town, Dave had left work early to start boarding up the windows on his waterfront home. He wasn't sure if the hurricane would actually impact their town, but he needed to play it safe.

He pulled up to his house, opened the tailgate of his truck, and pulled out some lumber. While setting up his table saw in the front yard, he looked up and down the street. Nobody else had boarded anything up. He was the only one currently preparing to do so. Why was that? Was he being paranoid?

While he was measuring the lumber and cutting it to size on the front lawn, his neighbor Chris came out to load something into his truck. "Hey, neighbor. What's going on? You building something?"

Dave stopped what he was doing and wiped the sweat from his brow. "I'm not taking any chances with this hurricane. I'm boarding up now while there's time still."

Chris chuckled. "Oh, that hurricane out in the Atlantic? I'm not worried about it. All of the weather guys I follow have said it's not hitting Cape May."

Dave put his hands on his hips and looked up at the quiet, misty gray sky. "I have this amateur meteorologist guy I follow. Younger fellow. He mainly does forecasts from his social media page. Maybe people might not think to follow someone like him, but let me tell you this: A couple years ago when we had that huge snowstorm, he forecasted it correctly when all of the weather people on the TV news didn't. Since then, he's amassed a huge following because people trust him. Now, he's saying it's going to hit Cape May in three to five days, contrary to what everyone else is saying. I have to go with my gut here."

Chris widened his eyes. "Oh, wow. Now you have me worried. I should probably start thinking about boarding up and prepping everything at the dock for the boat."

Dave nodded while picking up his extension ladder and leaning it against the house under a second-floor window. "Well, I've got the supplies for it. Just let me know. I can give you a hand if you need it, though I may be doing Margaret and Liz's B&B next. Nobody around here seems to be taking this storm seriously, though."

Chris scratched his head while looking at the neighbors' houses up and down the block. "I guess they don't follow your weather guy. Speaking of Margaret, you two still planning that wedding?"

Dave climbed halfway up the ladder, then stopped to look over at Chris. "Well, it seemed it may have been happening this year, but we couldn't decide on what kind of wedding, and now with this hurricane and her rushing around at the Seahorse, I don't know when we're going to get to plan or finalize anything. We might as well elope at this point," Dave said with a half-nervous laugh.

Chris chuckled. "I'm sure you'll come up with something, but I'll let you get back to what you're doing. I'm going to go follow your weather guy, in the meantime. Better safe than sorry."

* * *

That evening, Margaret got home from work and fell onto the couch in exhaustion after picking the girls up from Liz and Greg's. She laid on the couch and closed her eyes briefly.

A few minutes later, she felt a someone tapping her hand. "Mom. Mom, wake up," Harper said.

Margaret shook her head and looked around the room in confusion. "Oh, my. I must have fallen asleep. I didn't mean for that to happen."

Abby walked up next to Harper, wearing her riding britches and polo shirt. "Mom, did you forget about our horseback riding lesson tonight?"

Margaret sat up from the couch and looked at her watch. "Oh, wow. It looks like I did. Well, we still have some time to get there. Let me grab some snacks, and I'll meet you outside."

The girls ran out to the car, helmets in hand, just as Dave drove his truck into the driveway.

"Hi, Dave!" the girls bellowed as he stepped out of the truck and smiled.

"Hey, you two. Where's your mom?"

Abby pointed to the house "She's coming."

Margaret stepped out of the house, locked the door, and turned around to see Dave standing there with cowboy boots on.

Dave chuckled. "Why aren't you dressed for riding? Did you forget that we're all going on a trail ride around the property tonight?"

Margaret smacked her forehead. "Oh, that's right. I'll run back inside to change."

Dave smiled. "I'll drive. Just meet us at the truck."

When they finally arrived to the horse barn, they all took note of the ominous gray sky, but that didn't seem to stop Lexi, the instructor. The trail ride was still on with the group, and even some other parents were taking part.

Dave mounted his horse and watched as Margaret mounted hers. Meanwhile, Abby and Harper already sat atop their horses at the head of the line with Lexi, waiting with the other kids in the group to start the trail ride.

Margaret nudged her horse to move and nothing. "Come on, let's go, Bucky. We have a trail to ride."

Bucky turned his head to side-eye Margaret, then tried to nibble her foot.

Margaret sighed and looked at Dave. "I have a feeling I might be using a lot of leg on this ride. Bucky doesn't want to move."

Dave laughed. "Here, take my crop. You may not even need it. Just having one might get him to budge."

Sure enough, as soon as Margaret took Dave's crop, Bucky booked it.

Dave laughed again as he moved his horse faster to catch up to Margaret. "Hey you, let's hang in the back. We'll be the sweepers for this ride, and we'll be able to talk a little."

Margaret smiled and looked over at Dave riding the horse like he'd never stopped twenty-some years ago. "So, what do you want to talk about?"

Dave looked at the sky. "This hurricane, for one. My weather guy says he thinks it's coming for Cape May, but everyone else says it's bypassing us. But my guy is always dead-on with the forecasts. I boarded up most of the windows on my house today. I think I should do the windows at the Seahorse tomorrow."

Margaret sighed. "Really? That just seems like a lot of work, and nobody else on Beach Avenue has done it yet."

Dave shrugged. "Hey, I'm not a meteorologist, but I say better safe than sorry. I heard it's supposed to hit in three to five days. If we wait too long to board them up, then it might be too late. We can probably get away with just doing the front windows. It shouldn't take too long."

Margaret nodded. "I trust you. If you think I should, then I guess there's no harm. You'll be able to take them off afterwards, too?"

Dave chuckled. "Of course."

Margaret smiled at him as her body moved forward and backward with the horse's strong stride.

Dave looked over and smiled back. "It's nice out here, isn't it? I never knew I needed this back in my life. Aside from the frantic nature of this hurricane, I feel so at peace here. I'm glad we came."

Margaret looked around the property. The sun was on its way to setting beyond the tree line, and all was quiet aside from the chorus of crickets all around them. There was a slight chill in the air that made her wish she'd worn long sleeves, and a nearby campfire made everything smell like fresh fallen pines and smoky embers. It felt like heaven.

Dave took a long, deep breath, then looked out towards the tree line. "I know right now is probably not the best time to discuss this, but what are we thinking about this wedding of ours? Chris asked me about it earlier, and I really didn't have an answer to give him. I know we'd discussed getting married before the year is over. Do you still want to do that?" Dave asked with a hopeful heart.

Margaret thought for a moment, then turned to Dave. "You know, I was thinking about it so much, but lately I've been so busy at the B&B it has been drowned out. I think it might be best to push it until next year. I thought we would have some time to plan this month, but everything has been way too chaotic. I just don't see how we'd pull it off at this point."

Dave felt his heart sink as he watched the other riders turn right on the field, heading towards a small creek. "So, next year, huh?"

Margaret sighed and nodded. "There's probably no way we're going to find a wedding venue with a month or two's notice, not to mention a florist or a caterer. Will our guests even be able to come on such short notice? I'd like to take our time to really enjoy the wedding-planning process instead of rushing, you know?"

Dave made a half smile, trying to hide the disappointment he felt on the inside. Perhaps he'd made a big mistake telling Margaret he wanted a more traditional wedding while she'd hoped for something small and more intimate. At this point, he just wanted to marry her.

Margaret reached out her hand to hold Dave's. "I can't wait to marry you."

At that, Dave suddenly warmed on the inside and squeezed her hand as their horses walked next to each other in sync. "Ditto. For now, let's concentrate on this potential hurricane. I'm coming over to the Seahorse tomorrow."

CHAPTER FOUR

Liz and Margaret began another overcast day at the Seahorse, and aside from the loud bangs coming from outside where Dave boarded up some windows, it was pretty quiet.

Liz stared out the one window that wasn't boarded up yet. "So, Dave really thinks the hurricane is gonna hit here?"

Margaret walked up behind Liz and stared over her shoulder towards the ocean. "He swears by this weather guy he follows, and he said it's coming here. Just look at that ocean. The waves are rougher than I've seen in a while. Those surfers are getting tossed around like rag dolls."

Liz rubbed her eyes. "Is that Mom and Dad walking towards the house or am I imagining things?"

Margaret walked to the front door and opened it. "Looks like it is. Did they tell you that they were stopping by?"

Liz shook her head. "Nope. I'm guessing they didn't tell you either?"

Margaret rolled her eyes and laughed. "No, but you know how Mom is, she loves to be involved in everything."

Margaret watched as Judy and Bob walked up the porch steps, pausing briefly to watch Dave nail boards on the windows.

Judy got to the top of the porch first, followed by Bob, then smiled at Margaret and Liz, who were both now standing on the porch. "We thought we'd check in on you two with this hurricane coming. It may even start hitting tomorrow. Are you prepared?"

Before Margaret could answer, Dave stepped down the ladder after boarding up the last window, and walked up the porch. "Hi, Judy and Bob. You two doing OK?"

Bob smiled. "Oh, we're fine. I see you're helping out my girls once again. We thank you for that. I can't get up on those ladders like I used to. Doctor's orders."

Judy rolled her eyes, knowing full well a doctor never gave that order. "Dave, I'm glad you're being proactive. By the time the rest of the weather forecasters say the storm is definitely hitting Cape May, there will be quite a scramble to batten down the hatches. We follow Hurricane Sal on social media, and he's the only one saying it's coming here."

Dave nodded. "Yep. That's who I follow. Hence, why I'm doing all of this. I'm betting tonight the weather forecasters on TV will also be calling it."

Judy looked inside the inn from the porch. "Are your guests still here? Or did they go home due to the impending hurricane?"

Margaret sighed and looked around inside, spotting a few guests happily talking in the kitchen and a couple more reading in armchairs in the living room. "Well, they don't seem to be too worried about the storm, even with Sal saying that it'll hit here. I think they want to stay here and weather it so they can continue on with the monarch butterflies afterwards. Though I don't know how many of them will be around after the hurricane."

Bob shifted his eyes. "So, you're planning to ride the hurricane out here at the B&B, right across the street from the ocean? Is that safe?"

Margaret sighed and shook her head. "I'm not sure, but

what can I do? It's not like I can close the Seahorse while we have guests here. If it gets too bad, we can always figure something out, I guess?"

Bob looked around the B&B in thought. "Well, how about the girls stay with us tonight, then."

Before Margaret could answer, Judy announced that she was going to peek in the kitchen, and the next thing she knew, Judy screamed out.

"Marcy! What in the world are you doing here?" Judy bellowed as she walked over to hug her.

Marcy's eyes widened and her mouth dropped open. "Judy? Is that you? Am I dreaming? You look exactly the same!"

Judy waved her hand in the air. "Oh, stop! I do not."

Marcy stepped away from Judy and looked her up and down. "You do. I knew right away it was you even though I haven't seen you in what? Fifty-some years now?"

Margaret and Liz looked at each other, befuddled by the whole spectacle. "I'm surprised that Mom knows someone from Pittsburgh ... but then again, I'm not. She always seems to know someone wherever we go," Liz said as she walked into the kitchen.

Judy looked back at Margaret, Liz, and Bob who all stood in the kitchen watching. "We worked together at the ice cream stand on the Wildwood Boardwalk many years ago. Oh, and this is Bob, my husband, and Liz and Margaret are my daughters."

Marcy pointed at Bob with her mouth dropping open. "Wait a minute. Is this the guy who sang to you on the boardwalk while we were all working? The one who was relentless about asking you out on a date?"

Judy and Bob both laughed. "Yep, and I ended up marrying him. Can you believe it?"

Marcy laughed and shook her head. "It's so good seeing you again after all of these years."

Marcy's husband, Ed, got up to shake hands and introduce himself to Bob while Judy made herself comfortable at the kitchen table with Marcy and some other guests.

Margaret walked back out to the front porch where Dave stood with his hat turned backwards, arms folded, staring at the roaring ocean across the street, deep in thought.

"Hey, you. Whatcha thinking about?" Margaret asked as she stood next to him, studying the ocean as well.

Dave kept his eyes on the sea. "Hurricane Sal said the hurricane will most likely start hitting here tomorrow. There might be flooding, high winds, downed power lines. Who knows. I'm worried about you riding the storm out here."

Margaret gulped hard. She hadn't taken into consideration everything he just mentioned. By everything she had heard, it sounded like a bad storm that was going to pass over them. Evacuations were voluntary at this point. Nothing had been mandated.

"I think I'll be fine. I'm going to sleep over, just in case. We can't leave at night like we normally do. I need to be here in case anything happens," Margaret said as she looked up at the quiet dark-gray sky that felt like something out of a horror movie.

Dave turned to Margaret, enveloping her in a hug. "OK, I just want to know that you're safe."

Suddenly, the front door creaked up, and there in the doorway stood all of the guests staying at the Seahorse with Judy standing at the front.

Margaret shifted her eyes. "Mom … What's going on?"

Judy laughed. "I told them about a spot where I heard there was monarch butterflies, and well, we all want to go. I offered to drive some of them. Can you and Liz follow behind with the rest of the group?"

Margaret felt herself growing aggravated. "Mom, you realize that we're waiting for a hurricane to make landfall, right? I'm not so sure this is a good idea."

Judy stepped outside and looked up at the sky. "It's not coming for hours, maybe longer even. I really want to take them."

The group spilled outside and followed Judy to her car. Liz came out last, standing next to Margaret while rolling her eyes. "Well, Mom's at it again. I guess we have to do this now."

Margaret looked over at Dave for some kind of reassurance.

Dave held his hands up. "I'm letting you two handle this. I'll stay back and clean up my mess. Give me a call later," Dave said as he pecked Margaret on the lips.

Margaret sighed and walked inside to grab her purse and car keys. "OK, let's do this."

The three women ushered their guests into the cars and headed to the spot Judy knew about in Cape May Point by the dunes. After parking, Judy stepped out of the car, and the group followed her over to the dunes among the goldenrod and tall grasses in the sand.

"Well, this is where I was told they were. Hundreds of them. Maybe if we wait, they'll appear."

Liz looked up at the dark sky, which grew darker by the minute, and noticed the winds had picked up. The ocean waves had become stronger and louder as they smacked down on each other and the sand.

Suddenly, a woman in a rain jacket appeared as she walked off the beach and back to her car. "Gina?" Liz and Margaret both said aloud.

Gina did a double take. "Hey, you two. I just took some photographs of this insane ocean. What are you doing here?"

Margaret pointed to the group behind her. "We have guests at the B&B. They're here to see the monarch butterflies, and my mom thought right now would be a good time to see them. She heard of this secret spot."

Gina nodded. "I wish you'd told me. I've become very knowledgeable of these monarch butterflies. I used to drive down here from the city just to see them, and I learned all about them. I could give you some tips, but with this hurricane coming, all of the butterflies have instincts that tell them to hunker down. They're smarter than we give them credit for. They won't be out again until this hurricane passes."

Liz turned to their guests. "Did you all hear that? The butterflies won't be out until the hurricane passes, unfortunately. We should probably head back."

Just as Margaret and Liz turned back to Gina, the skies opened up and rain trickled slowly for a moment before quickly turning into steady sheets.

"Gina, get home safely. We're heading back now too," Margaret said as she unlocked the car with her key fob and ran.

While everyone piled into the cars, Margaret sat there in the driver's seat wiping rain off her face. Suddenly, she felt pretty uneasy at the prospect of staying at the Seahorse through the storm.

* * *

Across town, Dale had picked up Donna, who was still living at her parents, to take her to a fabulous "first date" surprise Italian dinner. A BYOB with the perfect romantic outdoor seating to enjoy the crisp air. However, the air was anything but crisp. It was rainy, windy, and dark outside.

Donna hopped into the car looking pretty in a tiered floral-print maxi dress complete with a long blue cardigan, and they were off to the restaurant.

Dale looked over at Donna and smiled. "You look gorgeous."

Donna blushed and waved her hand in the air. "Oh, stop it. You look great yourself. Where are we going?"

Dale smirked. "You'll find out as soon as we pull up."

Donna turned up the radio. "Can't wait."

As soon as Dale pulled the car up to the restaurant, Donna's eyes widened. "You didn't! I've been trying to get reservations here for a year."

Dale hopped out of the car, noticing there weren't any other cars in the parking lot. "Well, I'm guessing with this weather, maybe a lot of people aren't coming out for dinner tonight."

Donna walked with Dale to the door, where a sign was taped. *Closed due to incoming hurricane. Stay safe.*

Donna looked over at Dale, feeling confused. "I thought the hurricane wasn't hitting until late tomorrow? Are they getting a head start, I guess?"

Dale opened up his weather app on his phone. "I don't know. It's looking like it might hit earlier."

Donna stood there, as the mist turned to rain, soaking her beautiful dress and hair. "Well, what do we do?"

Dale looked back at his car. "Let's go back to my place. I have an idea."

As Dale made a break for the car, Donna received a text message alert. When she looked down, the word *Adam* appeared on the screen, making her stomach turn. She threw her phone into her purse, zipped it up, and ran to the car behind Dale, slamming the door shut before the rain soaked the interior.

Dale drove carefully through the storm, and after arriving home, he took off his jacket and held it over Donna's head as they both ran towards the front door. Once inside, they stood by the front door, water dripping off the both of them like a faucet.

Donna held her arms away from her body. "Do you maybe have sweat pants and a T-shirt I can borrow? I'm soaked."

Dale nodded. "Good idea. I'll get you some, and you can change in the guest room."

After Dale came back with a neatly folded pile of men's clothes for Donna to get changed into, she went to the guest room and shut the door. Standing in front of the mirror on the dresser, she assessed herself. Her makeup smeared down her face, her hair lay wet and flat. So much for a romantic dress-up evening.

Dale knocked on the door. "Would you like a towel to dry off with? I can leave it beside the door for you."

Donna, still staring into the mirror, ran her fingers through her wet hair. "Perfect, thank you, Dale," she said as she opened the door to take it.

She found a tissue from her purse and wiped her face, then held the towel to her face to feel the texture before rubbing it on her hair. Just then, another text message came through, reminding her she'd totally forgotten about the text Adam had sent.

This time, she quickly grabbed her phone and stared at the message. *Donna, are you OK? I'm worried about this hurricane. I'm staying at my buddy's place in Cape May. Everything just feels weird.*

Donna stared at the message for a full minute, not quite sure why Adam was texting her. He was scared of the hurricane? Well, why didn't he drive more inland and get a hotel somewhere? How does texting her solve anything?

Dale knocked on the door. "You OK in there?"

Donna looked at her phone one more time before changing into the sweatpants and T-shirt Dale gave her. "I'm good. Coming out now," Donna said as she stuffed the phone into the sweat's pocket.

Dale had lit some candles around the house, and had a movie on pause in the living room. In the kitchen, he'd begun whipping up something that smelled divine.

"What's all this?" Donna asked as she looked around at the homey ambiance before her.

Dale smiled while putting some garlic bread in the oven. "My idea of a cozy night in during a storm for our "first date." I'm making Italian food since we missed out on it tonight, and I found a riveting movie we can watch while we eat."

Before Donna could say anything, Dale reached up in the top cabinet and grabbed two wine glasses, and poured some wine into them. "Here you are. Go get snug in the living room, and I'll be in shortly with dinner."

Donna took a sip of her wine and shuffled to the living room, chuckling when she caught a glimpse of herself wearing a basketball team shirt and two-sizes-too-big sweatpants. Finding a nook in the sectional couch, with pillows where she could curl up, Donna got comfy. She pulled her phone out again in order to reply back to Adam.

Adam, what are you talking about?

Adam typed back immediately. *Hey, Donna. What are you doing?*

Donna looked at her phone in confusion. *Huh? What do you mean, what am I doing?*

Adam typed back. *Do you miss me at all?*

Donna stared at her phone in disbelief. *Is this a joke? Why are you texting me?*

Five long minutes went by with no response.

Dale walked into the room with two freshly made salads to start the meal. "Here you are. I used a lemon vinaigrette, is that OK?"

Donna smiled on the outside, still taken aback by Adam's text on the inside. "That sounds delicious. Thank you."

Dale had nodded and headed back into the kitchen to finish up dinner when Donna got another text message alert. She was afraid to even look by that point.

I just need to know. Do you miss me?

Donna stared at her phone, then promptly took it back into the guest room and put it in her purse.

She wasn't sure what was going on, but right now wasn't the time or place to be worried about it.

CHAPTER FIVE

Margaret stood on the front porch of the Seahorse early the next morning and watched as Hugh and Betty next door at the Morning Dew Cottage loaded up their car in a hurry.

Margaret took a sip of her coffee, looked out at the angry ocean and gray skies, then back at Hugh and Betty, who happened to catch a glimpse of her.

"Hey there, neighbor. Are you evacuating?" Hugh said while lifting the last piece of luggage into the trunk, then slamming it closed.

Margaret shrugged. "Well, it's not looking like it at the moment. The Seahorse is booked with guests."

Betty looked up at the dark sky and back at Margaret. "Well, if you stay, I'll cross my fingers that the Cape May Bubble will protect you. We aren't taking any chances. Growing up in Florida, I've endured my fair share of hurricanes, and I don't mess around with them. Stay safe."

Margaret nodded and waved goodbye as they pulled out of the driveway and turned out of site.

Cape May was considered a peninsula, surrounded by water on three sides. This somehow helped in keeping storms at bay in the area, and a lot of locals knew that, but many still didn't want to take a chance.

Margaret sipped her coffee, deep in thought, and then she suddenly realized that Dave had pulled up and was walking towards her.

"Hey, you," Dave said as he stood at the bottom of the stairs, taking off his hat and running his fingers through his hair.

Margaret snapped out of her thoughts and tried to crack a smile to mask the anxiety and worry that had started to overcome her. "Hey, Dave."

Dave, sensing something was amiss, cocked his head. "You OK? You look like you've seen a ghost."

Margaret set her coffee cup down and descended the porch steps to meet Dave. "I'm not sure. I just said bye to Hugh and Betty—they left in a rush. I'm starting to feel uneasy about staying here during the hurricane."

Dave rubbed Margaret's arm and turned to look at the roaring ocean across the street. "Well, can you tell your guests to go find another hotel inland?"

Margaret shrugged, feeling uncertain. "I don't know how well that's going to work out. One couple has dogs too, so that would make it even harder for them to find a place to stay."

Dave shook his head. "Do you allow dogs here?"

Margaret sighed. "No. They never asked. I'm allowing it this one time."

Dave chuckled. "Well, that was nice of you."

Margaret looked out towards the ocean again. "Do you want to walk on the beach with me? I'm both scared and mesmerized by Mother Nature right now. Those waves are insane."

Dave glanced at the ocean and shrugged. "Sure."

They crossed the street as the sky spat rain on the them and the clouds grew even darker. A few other people stood back to watch and catch photographs of the angry ocean.

Margaret and Dave stood near the dunes, and Dave wrapped his arms around Margaret as they both stared at the stormy waves.

Dave didn't say anything for a few minutes, but then abruptly blurted, "If you're staying at the B&B, then so am I. I'm not leaving you here alone."

Margaret shook her head. "I don't want to pull you into this, Dave."

Dave looked Margaret in the eyes. "Is Liz staying too?"

Margaret bit her lip. "Nope. I told her not to. She has the kids. My parents have my kids. It's better if I just be the one."

Dave swallowed hard. "Well, my house is boarded up too. I either stay in my house by the bay or here with you by the ocean. I could go stay inland with family or friends, but I'd be too worried about you."

Margaret squeezed Dave hard, then looked up at the sky. "Well, they're saying it's category one, right? It's supposed to start hitting early evening?"

Dave nodded. "That's what my guy says. I know a lot of old-head locals are riding the storm out and putting their faith in the Cape May Bubble. I guess they've seen it work its magic in the past, but there's no telling."

Margaret turned away from the ocean and looked out towards Beach Avenue. There were lots of businesses working fast to bring in tables, chairs, and umbrellas. The homes along the street seemed to have a lot of cars in the driveways and people on the porches still, though. It seemed everyone was preparing, but not everyone was voluntarily evacuating, which made Margaret feel a little better about her decision.

Dave followed Margaret's gaze. "How about we get inside? I packed a bag in my car and need to grab it. Is there anywhere for us to sleep?"

Margaret laughed. "Yeah, about that …"

* * *

A few hours later, the storm had picked up, and Sarah locked up and rushed out of the Monarch Coffeehouse, sheets of rain pummeling her. She'd let her employees leave earlier to get home to safety, so she was the last out.

As she fumbled with her keys, the rain drenched her until she finally unlocked the car door and heaved herself in. She took a moment to catch her breath before glancing at herself in the rearview mirror.

Shifting into reverse, the sound of her phone ringing startled her. She put the car back into park and answered the call. "Hello?"

"Sarah! You there?" Chris yelled into the phone, winds and rain whipping furiously around him as he exited his truck and stood on their front lawn.

"Chris, I'm here. What's up? I can barely hear you."

Chris stood outside of their house looking up at the dark sky. "My parents have offered to let us ride out the storm at their place. It's inland, and I think that might be better. I never got around to boarding up the windows due to work. What do you say?"

Sarah paused for a moment. She had only met his parents once before, during Sam's birthday party. And there had been so many people at the party that she'd barely had any time to really get to know them. She wasn't exactly feeling comfortable with a sleepover already.

Chris scrunched his brow and yelled through the loud winds and rain. "Sarah! You there?"

Sarah bit her lip. "Well … I guess that could work, but I don't know. You don't want to stick it out at the house?"

Chris glanced down the street at all of the boarded-up houses, his being one of the few that wasn't, then shook his head. "Yeah, I think we should take them up on their offer. Are you leaving work now? How about meet me over there. I'll text you the address."

Sarah gulped hard, feeling uneasy about everything in the moment. "OK, but I don't have anything packed."

Chris ran into the house, phone still in hand. "I'm at the house. I'll pack you some stuff really quick. I'll meet you over there shortly."

Before Sarah could get a word out, Chris had already hung the phone up, presumably so he could grab everything and get out quickly.

Sarah looked down at her phone and Chris's text came through with the address. She sighed, plugged the address into her GPS, then started on her way to his parents.

* * *

After a successful "first date" the night prior, Donna walked around her bedroom, tearing the place apart in search of her phone.

She'd scoured her car and the entirety of her parents' house, ultimately coming to the realization that she must have left it at Dale's last night. She quickly put her shoes on, hopped in the car, trying her best to dodge the wind and rain, and headed back to Dale's.

As she pulled into his driveway, Dale walked out the front door. He stood on the front step, concern written over his face.

Donna hopped out of the car and started walking towards Dale, the rain plastering her hair against her head. Just as she brushed some hair from her eyes, Dale's eyes grew big as he looked off into the distance over her shoulder.

"Oh, no! Donna, get in here *now!*"

Donna glanced back quickly to see what Dale was looking at, and in that instant, saw and heard a huge monstrous oak tree crack. It crashed onto the driveway, narrowly missing her car. She looked back at Dale and booked it towards the house.

Dale opened the door for Donna, but stood on the step for

a moment taking in what had happened before going inside, shutting the door behind him.

"Donna, are you crazy? Why are you out in this hurricane? You narrowly missed being killed by that tree."

Donna, not realizing how close she'd come, widened her eyes and ran to the window to look at what had just happened. Dale was right. It had only been a matter of seconds that she'd been standing in the exact spot where the tree had fallen.

Dale stood behind Donna, his arm around her even though her soaking wet shirt was plastered to her body. "You're stuck here now. Not only should you not leave again in this, but you literally can't. The tree is blocking the way out. Wait here. I'm going to get you some towels and dry clothes."

Donna walked to the kitchen, her whole body now shivering from the adrenaline pumping through her veins. She breathed a sigh a relief when she saw her phone sitting on the kitchen table. Though she'd assumed she'd left it there, she had not being completely sure. She picked it up, getting ready to call her parents when Dale walked in with a big fluffy towel, wrapping it around her, and hugging her tight.

"I heard hugging gets you dry faster," Dale said as rubbed Donna's arms under the towel and hugged her simultaneously.

Donna's whole body warmed over—and not just from the towel, but from Dale's touch. "Thank you, Dale. I guess it was pretty stupid of me to come out in this. I couldn't find my phone. I thought I had some time to come get it since the hurricane isn't even here yet."

Dale sighed. "Yeah, I noticed you left it here this morning, and I didn't have your parent's number. I figured you'd get it after the storm, but I can't say that I'm upset about you being here."

Donna smiled while toweling off her hair. "Guess we're stuck together, eh?"

A smile grew on Dale's face. "I've got a stocked fridge, and there are so many good movies and series out. I'll whip us up something good, and we'll hurricane it up. How about we start with a cheese board with homemade hummus and pita?"

Donna laughed while clutching her phone. "Sounds amazing. I have to call my parents to let them know I'm here."

Dale nodded while bending over to grab something out of the cabinet.

By way of greeting, Donna's mom breathed an audible sigh of relief while saying, "Where are you, Donna? You had us worried. A couple of trees went down in the neighborhood."

Donna could hear her dad talking in the background. "Mom, I'm fine. I shouldn't have gone out, but I left my phone at Dale's and needed to retrieve it. Now I'm stuck because a tree went down here too, blocking my car in …. Is Dad talking to someone?"

"Yes, he is, Donna," her mother said with a lowered voice. "Adam is here. They are talking in the living room."

"Wait. What? *Why* is Adam there?" Donna asked.

"Well, I'm assuming he came here to talk to you." Donna could imagine her mother shrugging. "Then when you weren't here, he ended up talking with us. We haven't seen him in a while. It's actually been nice to catch up, you know, even though you two are no longer together."

Donna put her hand on her forehead. "So, my ex decided to come talk during a huge storm and is now hanging with my parents during the hurricane? Shoo him out, Mom. This is unreal."

"Now, Donna, that is no way to treat someone. Him and your father are having a great conversation. Don't worry about it. We're fine. You be safe."

Donna ended the call and looked over at Dale, who was clueless about her whole conversation. She contemplated whether or not to tell him but ultimately decided that it probably wasn't the best time.

* * *

Sarah pulled up to Chris's parents' address and put the car in park. The rain pummeling down on the car, and her apprehension about going inside before Chris got there, made her sit in her car, deep in thought.

Fifteen minutes later, Chris parked behind her and ran into the house, not realizing Sarah was still inside her car. Sarah hopped out and ran inside behind him.

"Oh, there you are," Chris said while holding her packed bag and taking off his soaked hat.

Sarah shrugged. "I wanted to wait until you got here."

Chris smiled and pulled Sarah in close to him. "You didn't have to do that. My parents knew you were coming."

Chris's mom appeared from the kitchen. "Well, now. This hurricane is something, eh? Let me show you two to your rooms."

Sarah looked at Chris and mouthed, "Rooms?"

Chris's mom stopped at the first room. "This is where you'll be sleeping, Sarah, and Chris, you can stay in your old room. The twin bed is still in it. We're going to be eating dinner soon. Why don't you two get settled and meet us at the dining table in twenty minutes."

Chris's mom went back to the kitchen, leaving Chris and Sarah alone in the hallway.

Sarah rubbed her chin. "So, separate rooms, huh? Does she know we live together and share a bedroom?"

Chris sighed and shook his head. "Yeah, she knows. I don't know. I guess they're a little traditional and want us to be married before sharing a room."

Sarah laughed, a little too loudly at first. "But we already share a room."

Chris shrugged. "I don't know. I can't control my parents. It's one night. It'll be fine. I really don't feel like getting into it with them."

Sarah sighed and dropped her bag on the bed. "Well, you'd

better leave. I have to change. I wouldn't want you to see anything you shouldn't."

Chris nervously laughed, starting to realize that maybe staying at his parents' might not have been the best choice for them.

Twenty minutes later, they were all seated at the dining room table. The house was dead quiet except for the wind and rain outside and the old clock ticking on the wall.

Sarah stabbed at a pea with her fork, missing it the first five times before finally spearing it and popping it into her mouth. Everyone ate in silence. Not a peep was made my anyone. Even Chris sat staring at his meal, not looking up at Sarah or even engaging with her.

"So … the meal is quite good. Thank you," Sarah said as she looked around the table.

Chris's mom cleared her throat. "Why, thank you. It's an old recipe my mom used to make. It was Chris's favorite when he was growing up. Isn't that right, buttercup?"

Sarah had to conceal the laugh that threatened to erupt from her lips. Did his mother call a grown man in his forties *buttercup*?

Chris rolled his eyes. "Mom. I told you not to call me that anymore. It's … I don't know … odd."

Chris's dad, whose eyes had been glued to the muted television's newscast, slammed his hand down on the table. "Don't talk to your mother like that."

Chris stood up from the table abruptly. "I think I'm done here. I'm going to the basement."

Without a word to Sarah, Chris stormed off, leaving her awkwardly at the silent table with just his parents. She grew more uncomfortable and angrier with Chris by the minute. How could he have left her there with his parents to fend for herself?

She took her last bite and stood up with her plate. "Well, I'm stuffed. I guess I'll put my dish in the dishwasher?"

Chris's mom flicked her hand as if to say, "Go on," and Sarah rushed out of the room. She rinsed her dish, stuck it in the dishwasher, and walked down to the basement where Chris was.

"Chris! I'm hating this—I don't feel comfortable here. I'm ready to drive back to our house and wing the hurricane."

Chris sat down on a chair and buried his head in his hands. "I apologize for not warning you about my parents. I love them, but they can be unbearable. I really think you need to stay. It's too dangerous out there."

Sarah sighed and squeezed in next to Chris on his chair. Chris reached for her hand as they leaned into each other, going for a kiss. Right before their lips met, a voice came from the basement steps.

"Can you please not do that here?" Chris's mom said.

Sarah's stomach turned, anger burning up inside of her. She stood, looking from Chris to his mom. "You know what? I think I have another place to stay that will work out better. I'm going to get my bag and head out."

Chris immediately stood up and followed Sarah up the basement steps past his mom. "You can't, Sarah. It's too dangerous."

Once upstairs, Sarah grabbed her bag and whipped around to Chris. "I can't stay here. I will not stay here. Mark my words."

"Wait. I'm so sorry. I'll have a talk with my parents. I promise it will be fine. Please don't go," Chris said as Sarah walked outside into the rain.

Sarah turned around before getting in the car. "I'm going, Chris. I will lose my mind if I stay here."

Sarah slid into the car, backed out of the driveway, then took one last long look at Chris standing soaking wet on the pavement before putting the car into drive.

CHAPTER SIX

The hurricane was in full force by the evening. Dave and Margaret paced around the B&B while the guests played cards in the dining room with the television news broadcasting updates loudly.

"Dave, I'm growing more nervous by the minute," Margaret said as she opened the front door to heavy winds and sheets of rain. "The storm surge is already coming out onto the street. Look!"

Dave shook his head. "This is going to be a doozy. Let's hope we can get through this safely and with minimal damage."

Sharon and Ted walked down the Seahorse's stairs, and Dipsey and Doodle jumped out of their arms, running around the first floor, barking like crazy.

Sharon put her hands on her face. "My babies hate this weather. They're terrified."

Just then, Judy and Bob pulled their car into the driveway. They got out of the car immediately and ran up to the front door with a bag in hand and Hugo at their heels.

"Mom, Dad! What on earth are you doing driving in this? Do you see that storm surge across the street?"

Judy shook her head. "Your father insisted we bring this bag of flashlights over to you. He was worried."

Margaret sighed. "You didn't have to do that. We have plenty of candles."

Bob rolled his eyes. "These flashlights will be much better."

Margaret suddenly realizing her daughters weren't with her parents like they were supposed to be, started to panic. "Mom. Dad. Where's Harper and Abby?"

Bob slapped his knee. "That's right. I knew we had something to tell you…"

Judy cut him off. "They're fine. Liz and Greg have them. We were supposed to pick them up to take them to our place, but Liz said to leave them there. They're inland and they're having a ball spending time with Michael and Steven. She said to give her call whenever."

Margaret gave a sigh of relief. "OK. I'll do that. Thanks, Mom."

Another car appeared in the driveway behind Judy and Bob's car. Out stepped Sarah, who also immediately ran to the top of the steps.

Margaret and Dave looked at Sarah, then at each other in disbelief before ushering everyone inside into the foyer.

Sarah took off her rain jacket and pushed her wet hair out of her face. "Margaret, I'm desperate. I'm riding this storm out with you. I'll sleep in the hallway. I don't care. I needed to leave where I was."

Judy and Bob put their hand on Sarah's shoulders to comfort her. "Well, I'm sure Margaret could use some company, right?"

Margaret looked around the booked and busy B&B, then glanced at Dave and shrugged. "Sure, why not."

Sarah then looked over at Judy and Bob. "That road was almost flooded when I got here. I don't think you guys are leaving. Not to mention, I parked you in."

Bob shook his head. "Nonsense. We have some time." He

opened the front door to a now flooded Beach Avenue, water crashing onto the street from the ocean, and scattered outdoor chairs everywhere. "Well … maybe you're right," he said as he slammed the door closed.

Judy shucked her jacket and hung it on the coat stand. "Well, I guess we're riding this storm out here. Come, Hugo, let's say hi to everyone."

Sarah stood, adrenaline still coursed through her veins from everything that had happened. "I can't believe I drove in this. I must have been really desperate."

Margaret frowned. "What happened?"

Sarah started laughing. "The question is, what *didn't*. Chris's parents offered to let us stay at their house since they live inland. Let's just say it was awful. I had to get out of there."

Dave chuckled, which prompted Margaret to nudge him. "OK, I'm not saying a word. I'm going to look for more candles."

Sarah sighed. "Yeah, I don't really feel like getting into it right now. Chris is probably mad at me. I don't know. I may have even ruined our relationship. He got into it with his parents, and then, I somehow got dragged into the awkwardness of it all. It felt like we were in high school. They treated us like kids."

Margaret shook her head. "I'm so sorry, Sarah. I'm sure you and Chris just need to talk everything out. As for his parents, I don't know. I've been there and done that," she said with a laugh. "I have some extra clothes if you want to change in the basement and get dry?"

Sarah nodded, relief overcoming her as she followed Margaret to her bag of clothes. "Thank you, Margaret."

Suddenly, all of the lights went out. The guests in the kitchen panicked.

"I can't see!"

"Who's that?"

"Who am I touching?"

Dave came up from the basement. "Well, the good news is I found a boatload of candles. The bad news is I can't find a lighter or matches for the life of me."

Bob pulled a lighter out of his pocket. "Got one right here, Dave. Keep it on me in case the need for a nice cigar strikes randomly."

Dave sighed. "Great. OK, everyone stay put until we get the batteries in the flashlights and the candles lit."

Dipsey and Doodle ran over to Hugo, barking furiously. Hugo looked at them, yawned, and rolled over on his belly.

Meanwhile, Margaret helped Dave set the candles up around the first floor. "Dave, are we nuts for staying here?" she asked quietly.

Dave looked at Margaret's silhouette in the dark. "Honestly? Probably. We should have evacuated."

After all of the candles were lit around the downstairs, Margaret ran upstairs to get pillows and blankets. She arranged them in piles around the living room. "OK, everyone. Make yourself comfortable in the living room, kitchen, and dining area. Or upstairs if that's what you prefer. I've put out board games, books, and other things should you want to occupy yourself."

The guests shuffled around to different parts of the house, exploring the space in the dark, before they all somehow ended up together in the living room on the couches, chairs, and blankets on the floor. Sarah, Judy, and Bob joined them.

Margaret went into the basement to check on any flooding with her flashlight. In the pitch black, she shone her light around the room, the hurricane winds and rain being the only sound down there. Everything appeared dry. She hoped it would stay that way, but there was no telling. They hadn't owned the B&B during a hurricane before now.

She turned at the sound of footsteps coming down the steps, and found herself in Dave's flashlight beam. "You beat me to it," he said. "I was coming down to check if there was flooding down here."

He stood next to Margaret, so close that his arm hair prickled hers, giving her goose bumps.

Margaret bit her lip while shining her light around the room. "I guess we shouldn't have anyone sleep down here tonight in case it does flood, huh? Good thing I have all those extra blankets and pillows. We're having a good old-fashioned sleep over on the floor."

Dave nodded. "Yeah, I wouldn't risk it down here." He shined his flashlight towards the unfinished part of the basement, stopping by the washer.

"What's that?" Margaret asked, seeing his flashlight illuminate something behind the washer that reflected back.

Dave sighed. "I haven't a clue. You never noticed it before?"

Margaret shrugged. "No, can't say I have, though it is pretty far behind the washer. It's so gross back there that I try not to look with all the cobwebs and such."

Dave walked over and crouched down. "Here, hold my flashlight and light this area up for me. I want to see what it is."

A few hard, screeching tugs later, Dave had pulled out what appeared to be a large vintage film projector. "What on earth? How did we miss this?" Dave said as he held it up for Margaret to see.

Margaret's eyes widened. "Well now, that is cool. Are there film reels back there too?"

Dave set the projector down and turned back to look behind the washer. "Look at that. There is a film reel. Let's bring them upstairs to get them cleaned up."

They walked upstairs to find Judy had put together food for the guests while Bob loudly told stories to everyone in the living room with Hugo laying at his feet.

The wind outside got louder and louder, and Margaret

shuddered a little as she thought of what damage it could be doing.

Dave, now in his element, put the dusty old projector on the empty kitchen table and began cleaning it off with paper towels. He arranged sufficient light with nearby candles and held his flashlight between his teeth so he could use both hands.

Judy glanced over from the cheese and fruit tray she had put together. "Wow. I haven't seen one of these in years. Where did it come from?"

Margaret laughed. "Well, believe it or not, we found it behind the washer."

Dave fiddled with a few knobs and placed the film reel into the projector. "I can't wait to see what's on this. Too bad we don't have electricity."

Margaret walked out into the foyer, then looked into the living room. "Dave, right here on this hutch, pointing above the fireplace, may be the perfect place for it."

Dave came out with the projector and placed it delicately on the hutch with the film reel in place, plugged it in, then looked back to the spot above the fireplace. "That should definitely work."

Judy walked into the living room with her cheese tray, and everyone gratefully grabbed a paper plate, napkin, and some items off of it.

Margaret pulled a chair up to the group, making sure to plant herself next to Sarah. "How're you doing?" Margaret asked.

Sarah bobbed her head side to side. "OK, I guess. Things could be worse. I could still be at Chris's parents' right now."

Margaret gave a half smile. "Have you talked to Chris since?"

Sarah looked down at her phone in her hand. "He's called like five times. I should probably call him back, but I needed to cool down."

Margaret nodded. "I get that, but he probably wants to make sure you're OK. You ran out during a hurricane."

Sarah sighed. "You're right. I'm going to go call him now."

Sarah walked away from everyone and found a quiet spot in the kitchen.

"Sarah? Are you OK?" Chris asked after picking up right away.

Sarah took a deep breath and exhaled. "I'm fine, Chris. Look—"

Chris cut in. "Where did you go? I was so worried."

Sarah looked around the candlelit kitchen and out one of the un-boarded windows just in time to see a tree snap and fall down into the neighbor's yard. "I'm at Sarah and Liz's B&B. I'm staying the night here. I just watched the neighbor's tree fall down. This is unreal."

Chris shook his head. "Why did you go there? You're right by the ocean. That's no better than staying at home."

Sarah shrugged. "The Seahorse is boarded up, and everyone is here. We're making the most of it. I just couldn't stay at your parents' any longer."

Chris nodded. "I get it. My parents are difficult people, and I made the situation even more difficult for you when I left the dinner table. You have to know that I sincerely apologize. I love my parents, but they are not the easiest people to be around. They mean well underneath it all, though."

Sarah took a breath. "Well, thank you for that. I get it. Not everyone has picture-perfect parents. I guess I was taken aback. We've been dating for months, and I've only met them once, so I had no idea about any of this. A little warning would have been nice."

Chris walked back into the basement of his parents' house for privacy. "Well, I guess now you know why you've only met them once. I was afraid you'd get scared off and leave me," he said with a chuckle.

Sarah smirked. "Well, maybe they can come to our house

for dinner. You know, on our terms; where they can't make the rules."

"That would be nice," Chris said with a smile. "Maybe my sister and her family can come too."

Sarah paused for a moment. "Are you going to be OK there tonight? Has everything settled down?"

"I'll be fine," Chris assured her. "I think my parents are a little embarrassed actually."

Suddenly, the lights flicked back on in the kitchen, and the film projector clicked to life.

"Chris, let me call you later. Our electric is back on, which is odd since the storm is still raging," Sarah said as she walked around the house.

Dave immediately popped up out of his seat in the living and walked over to the projector. "We have power, and this old projector works!"

The lamps were turned off in the living room, and up above the fireplace, an old home movie projected onto the white wall.

Marcy and Ed, who were snuggled on the couch together with a blanket, dropped their mouths open at the same time. Outside, the winds and rain had slowed, and everyone watched what appeared to be a home movie from the seventies.

Dave sat down next to Margaret on the floor, propping his arm on a pillow, eager to watch the mystery reel.

Susan pointed at the movie, nudging Albert. "She's in a wedding gown, and it's here ... at the B&B. It's a wedding."

Marcy leaned back in her chair, bundling her blanket around herself. "Would you look at that. It's absolutely stunning."

Taking note that the wind had died down outside, Bob got up to open the front door and take a peek. "Would you look at that. Hey, everyone. I think we're through the worst of the storm. That hurricane was in and out in twelve hours. It seems to have passed, but the street and yard are still flooded."

Everyone got up to go see, stepping out onto the front porch.

Margaret and Dave were the only ones who remained in the living room, cuddled under a blanket on the floor, mesmerized by the beauty of the Seahorse all decorated for a wedding in the seventies.

CHAPTER SEVEN

The next morning, everyone awoke bright and early to head outside, eager to see what damage was done.

Margaret yawned and tried to adjust the kink in her neck from sleeping on the floor next to Dave while Bob opened the front door and walked out onto the lawn. He'd expected to see complete devastation. Instead, all he saw was a few shingles missing from the house, some huge puddles in the front yard, and lots of leaves and branches everywhere.

Dave walked outside and stood behind Bob, taking everything in. "Well, we got lucky. That's for sure. Not sure about everyone else in the state, though."

Bob nodded as he picked up a branch and tossed into a pile. "It's that Cape May Bubble, I tell ya. It's something."

The guests filed outside to assess the property. Marcy squinted her eyes as she stood on the sidewalk and looked up and down Beach Avenue. "Well, aside from some downed trees and debris everywhere, it looks like mostly everyone on this block got away unscathed."

Susan and Albert watched as a nearby business opened up their awning, and set out their tables and chairs out front. "The businesses are opening right back up. I say we help clean up around here. Do you have rakes and trash cans to put the debris in?"

Margaret nodded. "I do, but I don't want our guests to do that. We'll take care of it."

Marcy flicked her hand. "Nonsense. We want to help. It's the least we can do."

Margaret looked at Dave and shrugged. "Well, alright, if that's what you want to do. I'll go grab some yard tools."

Sarah walked up from the basement, having slept down there on the couch. She reported there wasn't any water damage, then asked, "How does everything look outside? Bad?"

Margaret shook her head and smiled. "Not really, thank goodness. Did you sleep OK?"

Sarah laughed while rubbing her back. "As good as anyone can on a recliner. Are you bringing those brooms outside? I can help."

Margaret smiled while handing her a broom. "If you want. The guests want to help clean. I'm going to grab more stuff from the shed."

A few hours of all-hands-on-deck cleanup, and everyone was famished. Margaret, with the help of Dave and Judy, was able to made a yummy meal out of the nonperishables. Unfortunately, everything else was going in the trash.

Sharon, with Dipsey and Doodle napping peacefully by her feet at the kitchen table, wiped her mouth after finishing her lunch and thought for a moment. "Well, I'm guessing the butterflies have been swept away by this hurricane. How could they possibly have managed to survive those winds?"

Everyone else was finishing eating and kind of shrugged, nobody really sure of how many monarch butterflies they'd end up seeing.

Just then, Irene, Bonnie, and Jackie showed up at the front door, hauling many bags of groceries. Jackie slammed two overloaded bags on the kitchen island. "Margaret, we heard the electric went out and figured you'd need more groceries."

Margaret put her hand over her heart. "Bless your hearts. You don't even know. Leave the receipt on the counter, and I'll reimburse you. I can't thank you enough."

Irene and Bonnie set their bags down and unloaded them into the fridge after tossing out what had gone bad.

Judy looked down at Hugo, who panted at her heels. "Well, now that everything is cleaned up and your help has arrived, I think we're going to head home. We still need to see what damage, if any, was done to our place."

The group said their goodbyes while Margaret plopped onto a chair in the living room, exhaustion from the last twenty-four hours overtaking her. Irene had followed her into the living room and eyed all of the blankets and pillows stacked neatly in a pile.

"Margaret, go home. We've got this. You don't need to be here," Irene said while looking around the room.

Margaret shook her head. "I can't leave yet. The guests helped clean up all of the storm damage, and I have yet to come up with a way for them to see any monarch butterflies, which is the whole reason they are here."

Jackie popped her head into the room. "They just survived a hurricane, I'm sure they'd like a nice peaceful day themselves. Go on."

Margaret looked at Dave, who nodded. "They're right. Let's get out of here."

Margaret hoisted herself out of the chair and grabbed her packed bag and purse. "Well, I do need to pick up the girls and check on Liz and Greg. Plus, we should see about our own houses."

* * *

When Donna and Dale awoke, it was not just to the one tree that had fallen, but two more as well. Donna stood next to the tree that blocked her car. "What are we going to do about this? Call someone?"

Dale thought for a moment, then turned and walked straight towards the neighbor's house.

"Where are you going?" Donna yelled after him.

Ten minutes later, Dale walked back with a huge chain saw. "Problem solved. Want to help me cut this tree up?"

Donna shook her head and laughed. "You with a chain saw? I never thought I'd see the day."

Dale cackled as the loud noise reverberated through the air when he fired up the chain saw. "I work with sharp knives for a living," he shouted. "I think I can handle this. Plus, my neighbor gave me the rundown on how to use it. I think I've got this."

Donna watched Dale lower the chain saw to the fallen tree trunk in the driveway, carefully slicing it into small manageable pieces, until her phone rang.

"Hello?"

"Donna?"

Donna walked towards the backyard, away from the chain saw's racket. "Adam?"

Adam took a deep breath. "It's me."

"Why were you at my parents' last night, Adam?"

Adam swallowed hard. "I don't know. I thought I'd just pop in and say hello."

Donna sighed with annoyance. "During a hurricane? Not to mention, you never wanted to talk to them the entire time we were married. My mom said you came to talk to me."

Adam cleared his throat. "Well, yeah, I guess. I've been texting you. Have you seen?"

Donna watched as Dale tossed a newly cut piece of tree trunk into the pile he had made. "I have, Adam. I just haven't known how to respond. We're divorced now, in case you haven't noticed."

Adam laughed nervously. "I have noticed."

Donna bit her lip. "And should you really be texting your ex-wife these things when you're dating someone else? Jen from the other softball team?"

Adam nodded. "Probably not. She doesn't compare to you, Donna. I miss you. I want you back. I lied. I didn't come back for Jen. I came back for *you*."

Donna stood up. "Whoa, whoa. whoa. Back it up there, Adam. I wasn't happy in our marriage, remember? I'm with someone else now."

Adam rolled his eyes. "That guy that runs the funnel cake stand? He seems like a real winner."

Dale caught Donna's eye, and he smiled and waved. Donna hesitated before slowly waving back, still digesting what Adam was saying.

Adam laughed. "OK. Well, I guess I'll go. Take care, Donna."

Donna hung up the phone, feeling a mix of emotions rise up in her. Like her friends suspected, he came out to Cape May from California for *her*. It was fine, though. He had mentioned he was only here for a couple weeks. He'd be gone soon and would be a distant memory again.

Sarah drove back to the home she shared with Chris to find him already there doing yard clean up. His radio blared, and Sarah could tell by the tension in his shoulders that what he was doing wasn't only about yard cleanup but also letting off some steam.

Chris took a large tree branch and stepped on it, loudly cracking it in half before tossing it (with force) to the other side of the yard. He quickly looked at Sarah before going back to what he was doing.

"Hi," Sarah said over the loud cracking noises.

"Hi," Chris said coldly, not even turning to look at her.

"Do you need help?" Sarah asked, looking around the debris-strewn yard.

Chris gave a sarcastic laugh. "Do I need help? No, thanks. I think I can handle this."

Sarah narrowed her eyes. "Why are you talking to me like *that*?"

Chris threw another log to the side. "Like what?"

Sarah shook her head. "I'm not playing games, Chris. Fine, I'm going inside."

Chris yelled out to her as she walked away. "I'll tell you why I'm acting this way. It's because of you. You scared me half to death last night. It wasn't right."

Sarah whipped herself around. "I get that, but you know what scared me even more? Being stuck at your parents any longer. Next time, don't abandon me at the dinner table and leave me to fend for myself. How about that?"

Chris wiped the sweat off his brow. "But did you have to leave? Couldn't we have just talked it out?"

Sarah laughed. "Talked where, Chris? When we started to talk in the basement, your mom came down. There wasn't anywhere for us to talk privately, and heaven forbid we went into a bedroom together to talk."

Chris sighed. "I get it. I really do. We should have figured out a backup plan besides my parents' house. And now I know for the future, but what you did … it gutted me. How was everything at the B&B?"

Sarah took her brown hair out of her ponytail and let it cascade down past her shoulders. "Aside from the kink in my neck from sleeping on a recliner, it went pretty well, actually. There was a lot of people there, and it was quite fun. We talked, we laughed, we ate some good cheese."

"Well, OK, then. It certainly does sound nice. I just wish

we could've talked it out. If this is going to work, we need to have better communication," Chris said as he went back to tossing branches.

Sarah looked off towards the water. "True, but if this is going to work, we need some boundaries with your parents. I don't ever want to go through that again."

* * *

Dave and Margaret pulled up to Liz and Greg's, taking notice that the farm was pretty torn up.

"Mommy!" Abby and Harper yelled as they ran out of the front door, the screen door banging loudly behind them.

They hugged Margaret tightly while Dave ruffled their hair.

"Hi, Dave!" Abby exclaimed as she turned to him for a hug.

Dave picked her up and twirled her around. "How did you two make out last night?"

Harper's eyes widened. "It was pretty scary to hear the winds, but we mostly played video games with Michael and Steven."

Liz and Greg walked outside, Liz rubbing her arms against the chill in the air while Greg walked over to Dave to shake his hand. "How was everything over at the Seahorse? OK, I hope?"

Dave and Margaret nodded. "Actually, not much damage at all. Just some yard debris and a few loose shingles. We cleaned a lot of it up today."

Margaret smiled. "And the guests insisted on helping. It was a nice team effort. How did you guys make out?"

Liz bit her lip. "Well, go take a look at the farm."

Margaret looked at Dave and widened her eyes. "Oh, no."

They walked to the backyard to see all of their trellises

flung around the garden. The covered decking they'd built had been ripped apart, and everything was in disarray.

"Oh, this is *not* good," Dave said. "Though, it's nothing we can't fix."

Margaret eyed a cluster of orange on some of the flowers that were still blooming in the wildflower patch. "Wait, what is that?"

The rest of them squinted their eyes. "It looks like some orange flowers. What kind did you grow? They seemed to survive this storm pretty well."

Margaret shook her head and walked towards them. "No, it's not flowers. It's moving."

As Margaret got closer, she saw, plain as day, the elusive monarch butterflies. The ones her guests traveled hours to see, though they really hadn't seen them at all yet.

Dave, Liz, and Greg walked next to Margaret, following her gaze.

"You're kidding! Are those the monarch butterflies we've been stressing about finding" Liz asked.

"Yes!" Margaret said as she whipped out her phone to take pictures.

Dave looked around the garden, taking in everything that had to be done, ultimately stopping at the monarchs everyone was staring at. "I have an idea that I think will work nicely for everyone, including your guests."

Margaret's heart leaped. "Are you thinking what I'm thinking?"

Dave nodded. "Yes, but think bigger."

Margaret furrowed her brow. "What do you mean?"

"Let's see if our friends might want to help clean this farm up. Afterwards, we can get something to eat with everyone and discuss how we can give your B&B guests what they came for. I'm thinking everyone will have some unique ideas of their own."

Liz and Greg nodded. "Sounds like a great idea to me. I'm sure I can come up with something," Greg said happily.

Liz put her arm around Greg. "I'm liking the sound of this Dave."

Margaret smiled while looking back at the butterflies. "I think that sounds like a great idea, and we already have our own private butterfly viewing spot right here."

CHAPTER EIGHT

Dave's plan became reality overnight. Sure enough, the next day, Donna, Dale, Sarah, Chris, and of course Margaret, Liz, and Greg were able to help out on the farm for a couple hours putting it all back together. After washing up, they all went out for lunch at the Lobster House.

After everyone ordered, yummy dishes started making their way to the table. Lobster bisque, clam chowder, Cape May scallops, crab cakes, and lobster tail. It was a feast of feasts.

Dave clinked his glass. "Hey, everybody. Thank you so much for helping out today on the farm. Not only was it productive, but fun too. Over at the Seahorse Inn, you may or may not know that guests came in from Pittsburgh and rode the hurricane out at the B&B. They, then, helped clean up after the hurricane, even helping some neighbors. We really want to make the rest of their time here special."

Margaret nodded. "They came to see the migrating monarch butterflies, and they've been here nearly a week and haven't seen *any*."

Liz took a sip of her drink and cut in. "Does anyone have ideas for how our Pittsburgh guests can see monarch butterflies and/or learn about them? We're desperate for ideas or activities. They have about another week left here, and we want to make it count."

The entire table started trying to gather ideas.

Dave cut in. "I'm going to throw my idea out that I got yesterday. The farm we all just cleaned up seems to be attracting monarch butterflies."

Sarah smiled. "That's right. I saw a few while we were out there working today."

Dave nodded and smiled. "Well, I was thinking of taking the Pittsburgh guests there tomorrow. Let them watch the monarchs, give them a tour of the garden, and let them take part in the harvest process. We have plenty of fall crops like carrots, beets, lettuce, radishes, and peas."

Margaret squeezed Dave's hand under the table. "That sounds amazing."

Sarah chimed in. "I'm loving that idea, Dave. I think I've got something to bring to the table. I was thinking of making a themed hot drink over at the Monarch Coffeehouse. Maybe even bring in an educational speaker to discuss the monarch butterflies, though I don't know where I'm going to find one."

Liz's eyes widened. "I love that!"

Chris cleared his throat. "Would they be interested in a boating tour to see the shorebirds? Maybe I can meet them at the hawk-watching platform to observe the migrating hawks as well? I don't have much experience with butterflies, but there's also another big migration going on in Cape May right now with the bird world."

Margaret nodded. "I think that sounds great. I'll ask them. I guess I'll throw in my idea now. I was thinking of taking them to the Cape May Meadows and Garrett Family Preserve to try and spot them."

Greg raised his hand. "How about I put together a monarch-themed dinner over at Heirloom?"

Liz smiled. "Sounds perfect."

Donna and Dale looked at each other. "We're not sure what we can contribute, but we'll think on it."

Liz clapped her hands. "I think this is going to work out wonderfully. We have a few more days to fill, so hopefully we figure some more stuff out."

The table went back to eating, drinking, and talking about other things as Margaret felt her heart warm over at the thought that Dave got the wheels moving on all of this.

* * *

After lunch, Sarah stopped in to check on things at the Monarch Coffeehouse. It was their first day open since the hurricane, and she wanted to make sure everything was running smoothly.

Dawn greeted Sarah as soon as she walked in. "Hey, Sarah!"

Sarah smiled while glancing around the coffeehouse, her eyes stopping on the same woman on her laptop in the corner that had been there before the hurricane. The one, who always seemed to be observing everything and everyone in the coffee-house more than anything.

Dawn followed her gaze. "Oh, yeah. Our regular is back at it. As soon as we opened, she was one of the first people that came in."

Sarah smiled. "Well, I guess she likes it here."

Dawn chuckled. "I guess."

"So, how are you making out? Has it been slow?" Sarah asked while still looking around the shop.

Dawn laughed. "Um, no. Not at all. I think everyone was desperate to get out after the hurricane. We had a line out the door earlier."

Sarah put her hand over her mouth. "Are you serious?"

Dawn flicked her hand in the air. "Don't worry. It went smoothly. No one had to wait more than five minutes. We were pretty speedy in making their drinks. We even sold out of most of the pastries," Dawn said as she pointed at the bare case.

Sarah sighed in relief, then looked around again, her eyes stopping on the regular immersed in her laptop sitting in the corner. "OK, good. I just stopped by to check on things, but I can see you have everything under control. You know, I think I'm going to talk to that woman that's always here."

Dawn's eyes widened. "Are you sure? She always seems like she prefers to be … unbothered."

Sarah bit her lip. "Call me crazy, but I'm going to do it."

Dawn cocked her head and took a deep breath. "Well, I'll cross my fingers for you, Sarah."

Sarah nodded and headed towards the woman in the back corner, who quickly took notice. She glanced up at Sarah, then quickly averted her eyes back to her laptop.

"Hi, there. I'm Sarah, the owner," Sarah said as the woman typed furiously.

Finally, after several long moments, she stopped typing and looked up. "Oh, hi. Lovely place you've got."

Sarah chuckled. "Well, we see you here all of the time, and I thought it would be proper to introduce myself."

"Nice to meet you," the woman said, resuming her furious typing and locking her gaze to her laptop screen.

Sarah nodded. "Well, I'll let you get back to what you're doing." Sarah started to turn and walk back to the coffee counter.

"Wait," the woman said.

Sarah's eyes widened as she turned around.

The woman sighed as she shut her laptop. "I'm sorry. I haven't exactly been polite. I'm Christine," she said as she held out her hand.

Sarah shook her hand. "Great to meet you, Christine."

Christine sighed deeply. "I have all these crazy deadlines. It's why I am how I am. I do want to thank you for allowing me to work here. I buy drinks and such, of course, but I still take up a table for the better part of the day."

"That's completely fine. It's how things are at coffeehouses," Sarah said happily.

Christine looked at Sarah, her heart heavy. "Look, I need to be honest with you. I'm writing a review for the local paper. I started coming here to write a review on the Monarch Coffeehouse."

Sarah's eyes widened. "Really? Has the review come out yet?"

Christine shook her head. "Not exactly."

"What do you mean?" Sarah asked.

Christine sighed. "Well, I kind of submitted a bad review to be published in this Sunday's paper. But then, I realized I'd caught this establishment on an off day, as everything has been amazing since. I asked my editor not to run it, but I haven't heard back. I'm afraid it may have been too late. I'm so sorry."

"Oh, no," Sarah said as she held her hand to her mouth. "You must have based your review on the day I was training my new staff."

Christine nodded. "Yep. I realized that after I submitted it. I feel horrible."

Sarah glanced around the room. "Are they sure it's too late to change it?"

Christine bit her lip. "I'm going to try my hardest to make sure it's not published. I really love your establishment. It's why I have been back since. I came here to review the place, and after that one bad day, I learned to really love it. It's so much easier to work here than at home too. Oh my gosh, I feel horrible."

Sarah slumped down in the chair at the other end of Christine's table. "It's fine. I mean, if the review gets published, it is what is. I guess all places get *some* bad reviews. What are you working on now?"

Christine opened her laptop and looked at her screen. "I'm working on a piece about the monarch butterflies."

Sarah's eyes widened. "You're kidding!"

Christine laughed. "No, am I not. I guess you like them considering the name of your coffeehouse."

Sarah laughed. "Yes, but I don't know a ton about them, and I'm actually looking for someone to do a talk on the butterflies this week. Do you think that's something you could do?"

Christine swallowed hard. "Well, I hate speaking in front of people, but … I feel I owe this to you."

Sarah smiled. "Perfect. I'm doing a favor for a friend. She will be thrilled."

Christine cocked her head to the side. "Really? I'm intrigued."

"She has a group at her B&B that traveled specifically to see the monarch butterflies during migration, and let's just say the hurricane hasn't helped that," Sarah said.

Christine scratched her head in thought. "I think I've got the perfect presentation idea."

* * *

Margaret pulled into a parking lot in downtown Cape May, and after she parked, she looked over at Dave in the passenger seat.

"I'm taking you to this wonderful old bookstore. Maybe you've been before?" Margaret asked.

Dave shrugged. "Honestly, I don't remember."

They walked down the little alleyway to The Book Nook, the bell on the door announcing their arrival as they opened and shut it. Sampson, the black cat, was perched atop the counter with the register this time, and gave a little purr when they walked in.

Dave immediately walked over to Sampson and gave his head a pet.

Margaret smiled. "I thought you weren't a cat person?"

Dave laughed. "Well, I'm not, but I do love animals."

Margaret's heart warmed as she moved next to Dave to pet the now-happy-as-a-clam cat.

Dave sighed. "Joan is fostering those kittens that Butch had. They should be ready for homes soon once she gets them fixed. Were you still thinking …?"

Margaret's eyes twinkled. "Of getting our first pet together? Sort of."

Dave smiled as he scratched under Sampson's chin, and he rolled onto his belly. "Well, I'll talk to Joan about it."

Margaret smiled and took a deep breath of the old book smell that permeated the room. "Well, what do you think of this place? It's great, isn't it? I used to come here with my father as a kid."

Dave stopped petting Sampson to wander around and take it all in. He ran his fingers over the books on a shelf, stopping on one. He grabbed it and flopped into a Victorian loveseat before opening it and flipping through the pages.

Margaret found another book on butterflies and squeezed in next to Dave. "Whatcha readin'?"

Dave turned the cover of the book to himself and said, "*The Beginner's Guide to Impromptu Weddings.*"

Margaret laughed. "That's really what it's called?"

Dave shook his head and smiled. "No, it's an old copy of *The Secret Garden*, but I really feel like we should be reading about impromptu weddings. Are you sure you want to wait until next year to get married?"

Margaret scrunched her brow while flipping through her book's pages, not really paying attention to them. "I mean, we probably would have a much nicer wedding if we waited until next year sometime. How do you feel about waiting? I assumed you'd be all for it so we can plan that big, magical day you want."

Dave sat up, ready to tell Margaret everything he felt just as a woman walked out from the backroom.

"Gina?" Margaret asked, confused.

"Margaret! Hey, girl. What are you doing?" Gina asked excitedly.

Margaret stood up from the couch. "I had to show Dave this quirky bookstore that I've rediscovered. I simply love it here. Do you work here?"

Gina laughed. "Oh, no. My father owns this bookstore. I just fill in here and there to help out."

Margaret's eyes widened. "Well, what a small world. You remember my fiancé, Dave, right? I think you met over at Mayer's Tavern not too long ago."

Dave got up and shook Gina's hand.

"Well, good to meet you again. Is there anything I can help with?" Gina asked with a smile.

Margaret sighed while looking around the room. "Not really. I mean, maybe. We have this Pittsburgh gardening club staying at the B&B, and they're here to see the monarch butter-flies, and well, that kind of got disrupted by the hurricane. I guess I'm trying to gather some ideas. I was thinking about maybe bringing them here, but—"

Gina eyes twinkled as she clapped her hands. "I have the perfect idea. Better than here."

Margaret nodded. "Really? What are you thinking?"

"The Monarch Butterfly Festival, of course!" Gina said.

Margaret furrowed her brow. "What are you talking about? Where is that?"

Gina laughed. "Here, you silly. In Cape May. You don't know about it?"

Margaret laughed. "No. I've never heard of it, and I've lived here my entire life."

Gina shook her head. "Margaret, Margaret. What are we

going to do with you? How about this. Bring them to the festival this Saturday. I'll meet you there at my tent. Then, afterwards I'll take you all to my secret spot over in Cape May Point."

Margaret's heart swelled two sizes. She gave Gina a huge hug and said, "You just put the final touches on a week of monarch activities for our garden club tourists. I've been stressing myself out trying to find things for them to do. Between everyone involved, I think we really have this covered."

Dave, who had walked out of the room and into another room of the library, walked back in the room holding the black cat who purred like a baby in his arms. "What did I miss?"

Gina laughed. "So, you like Sampson, eh? He can be a little ham."

Margaret smiled. "Oh, you only missed Gina telling me about the Monarch Butterfly Festival this weekend. How did none of us know about it? And after all these years?"

Dave shrugged, still holding Sampson. "I discover something new about Cape May every day. It's part of what makes this shore town so intriguing."

CHAPTER NINE

A few days later, Dave stood before their farm on Liz and Greg's property and took a deep breath as the sun rose over the tree line in the distance. A misty fog laid low to the ground, and everything felt serene and quiet.

Liz walked outside with two steaming mugs and stood next to Dave. "Coffee?"

"Thanks, Liz," Dave said as he took a satisfying sip.

Liz gazed over the landscape. "What time are they all getting here?"

Dave glanced at his watch. "Any moment now. I'm kind of nervous. I hope the butterflies make an appearance."

Liz nodded. "Same, Dave. Same."

Just then, Margaret, Bonnie, Irene, and Jackie's caravan of vehicles pulled into the driveway carrying the Pittsburgh visitors. When they had flooded out of the cars and walked over to Dave, he smiled. "Good morning, everyone!"

The group yawned and waved while Sharon, toting her designer bag and fancy shoes, let Dipsey and Doodle out in the grass to run around.

Margaret walked up next to Dave and touched his back. "How's everything? Are you ready for your big plan?"

Dave chuckled. "I guess, but are *they*?"

Margaret looked back over at the very tired faces. Then, she glanced at Liz with a confused face.

A light bulb went off in Liz's head. "I have a pot of coffee inside. Does anyone want a cup?" Everyone's eyes lit up with excitement, and it was then Margaret remembered that nobody had time to drink a cup of coffee at the Seahorse.

Once everyone was caffeinated, Dave led the group back outside. "So, this is our farm. Margaret and I created this garden last year here on Liz and Greg's property. Over there is our farm stand, which we call The Cape May Garden. I thought I'd give you a tour of the property, let you harvest some things if you'd like, then show you the spot where the monarch butterflies should be."

The group nodded, softly conversing with each other.

Dave looked at Margaret nervously. "Wanna help me? I'm not sure where to begin here."

Margaret laughed. "You got it. OK, everyone, follow us, and make sure to look where you're walking. We cleaned up after the storm, but you never know what might have been missed."

The group followed behind them, getting a good look at the row crops of red, yellow, and candy-striped beets, carrots of all sizes and colors, vibrant green lettuce, kale, and cabbage.

Dave stood next to a trellis growing peas, and plucked off a few plump pods. "Anyone want some of nature's candy with your coffee?"

Most everyone grabbed a pea pod, opened it up, and popped the sweet peas into their mouths.

"That really is nature's candy," Marcy said as she savored the fresh flavor. Right off the vine couldn't compare to what she was used to getting in the grocery store—it stood head and shoulders above that produce.

Margaret pulled a few French breakfast radishes out of the ground, then walked over to the hose and washed them off.

"Most of the crops we're showing you grow best in the cooler temperatures of fall and spring. I've tried to grow these radishes in the summer, and the flavor is extremely spicy. Now, though, is a different story. They should be quite good. Here's a few if anyone wants to try them," Margaret said as she took a bite.

A few people took a radish and nodded as they bit into them, savoring the crisp flavor. After another hour of showing the group around the garden, which they seemed to really enjoy, they got to the flower field full of late blooming sunflowers, zinnias, nasturtium, and cosmos.

Dave scanned the field, trying to zero in on the spot where he'd seen the butterflies days prior. "OK, for the grand finale, we should be able to see the monarch butterflies in this flower field."

After ten minutes of standing and not seeing anything but the flowers, the group started getting antsy. Margaret took notice of the stack of Adirondack chairs next to their covered deck area by the field. "Would anyone like a seat while we wait?"

Sharon looked down at her fancy but uncomfortable shoes. "Yes, please. That would be great."

The rest of the group nodded as well. After getting the seats situated by the flower field, everyone seemed content again, that is until …

Slap! "Ow!" *Slap! Slap!* Joyce swatted at the bugs that swarmed all around her.

Everyone else looked around themselves, taking notice of the little bloodsuckers sitting on their arms and legs, and began furiously slapping them off.

Dave shook his head. "Well, I thought it was going well for a moment there …."

Margaret looked at him lovingly, giving a half smile. "You've done a great job. You can't control the bugs."

As Sharon smacked away the pests, Dipsey and Doodle ran

out of her arms and across the flower field, making a beeline for the thick trees.

Ted's eyes widened. "Dear! The dogs have run away. They never go that far from us."

Sharon stopped swatting and started running in her fancy shoes across the field towards them, Ted following behind.

Susan and Albert looked at the rest of the group and stood up from their chairs. "Well, I guess we'd better help them. Maybe we'll get away from the bugs in the process."

Everyone groaned as they got up and followed the pair out past the flower field towards the tree line. Sharon and Ted were far ahead, yelling out to their escaped dogs.

Margaret, Dave, and Liz joined in as well. Eventually, Sharon and Ted disappeared out of sight but could still be heard inside the forested area.

Everyone caught up to them right by the tree house that Dave had built for the kids. Sharon and Ted each grasped onto a dog tightly while catching their breath.

"Thank goodness you got them," Marcy said as she looked around at the beautiful patch of forest that they now stood in.

Sharon sighed as she pet Doodle. "Maybe we should have left them back at the B&B."

Ted cut in. "Or maybe you should have brought their carrier like I suggested. They are too tiny to be running off."

Susan and Albert walked to the little stream that ran by the tree house and kneeled down to touch the water before standing up to look ahead at something off in the distance.

Dave followed their gaze to see a smattering of orange— monarch butterflies flying above them. "There they are. The monarch butterflies."

Everyone turned to look, finally seeing the beautiful insects they had waited so long to catch a glimpse of. They stood in awe watching the butterflies flutter above them, taking a moment to really enjoy the sight before popping out their phones to take photos.

After fifteen minutes or so of observing, everyone headed out of the forest and back towards the flower field when lo and behold, the spot where Dave had seen the butterflies now had a bunch.

They all quietly watched from a distance as the monarchs sat atop the many colorful flowers. It was a small cluster of them, but still beautiful to watch, nonetheless.

Dave grabbed Margaret's hand and gave it small squeeze and smiled at her, knowing the relief they both felt.

* * *

Chris started the boat as the Pittsburgh guests, along with Margaret, Dave, Liz, Judy, and Bob, boarded their own private sunset birding tour. Chris let everyone take a seat as he backed the boat out of the dock and into the inlet towards the bay. "OK, everyone. I'm Chris, the owner of this boat. I give regular birding tours. In the middle row of seats you'll find binoculars. Please grab a pair so you can get a better look at what we come across."

Everyone got up to pick a pair from the pile, then sat back down on the cushioned row seating. Margaret touched Dave's hand as they sat staring out the open windows of the interior area of the boat. "Let's go stand over there."

They walked out to the open-air deck in the front of the boat, binoculars around their neck, and leaned against the railing, letting the fresh air whip them in the face as the boat picked up speed. Neither of them had been on one of Chris's birding boat adventures before.

Dave pointed to a cluster of birds, which Chris must have noticed since he subsequently slowed the boat to a stop.

"Over here we have some black skimmers," Chris said as he put his binoculars up to his eyes to get a better look. "Right about three o'clock there."

Before Chris was able to detail the migrating pattern of the black skimmer, all of the guests squeezed out onto the small decking area at the front of the boat alongside Margaret and Dave. Everyone, that is, except Marcy who was using the bathroom at the back of the boat, and Joyce who stood waiting to use it too.

Everyone watched the birds with their binoculars while packed in like sardines on the front deck when the bathroom door could be heard opening in the back.

"Uh, Chris, is it?" Marcy asked as she walked towards the front of the boat.

Chris lowered his binoculars. "Yes?"

Marcy cleared her throat. "We have a little issue. There's something wrong with your bathroom door. As I exited, I shut it behind me, but now Joyce can't get it back open."

Chris took a long sigh. "Really? I just fixed that issue. Here, let me try."

Joyce stood off to the side with her legs crossed, trying to conceal how badly she had to go. Chris took ahold of the door and pulled a few times. Then, Dave came back and gave it some extra manpower. Nothing.

Chris sighed. "I think the inside lock somehow must have gotten latched when it shut. I won't be able to fix this until we get back."

Marcy looked over at Joyce, who stood there looking very uncomfortable. "I think Joyce really has to go."

Joyce nodded while scanning the boat.

Chris walked back to the wheel. "That's totally fine. We're only about ten minutes from the dock. There's a bathroom there. I'll head over now."

Ten minutes later, they were back at the dock, and a few people left to use the bathroom, then they were back on the boat and ready to go towards the bay again.

Chris stood behind the wheel as he maneuvered the boat out of the dock, when an idea came into his head. Dave stood next to him, observing some of the ins and outs of driving a boat.

"A friend of mine told me about this little secret shortcut through the marsh that I've been wanting to check out. I'm going to try it out," Chris said to Dave as he turned the boat around.

Dave nodded, while glancing over at Margaret, who happily chatted away with everyone on the front deck while Chris pulled the boat into a little alcove and slowly maneuvered it forward.

When everyone at the front of the boat pointed to the left, Chris asked, "What does everyone see?" as he stopped the boat and looked out the window.

There before him, along the marshes, were hundreds of old vintage glass bottles. It was a sight to be seen.

Dave poked his head out the window next to Chris's. "Wow. Do you think the hurricane uncovered all of this?"

Chris nodded. "I certainly do. These look like rare artifacts. Maybe from an old shipwreck. Who knows."

The guests overheard their conversation from the deck as they oohed and aahed over the beautiful bottles.

"You really think these might be from a shipwreck?" Sharon asked curiously.

Chris shrugged while getting up to grab a big net from the back wall. "Possibly. I'm going to try and grab a few to see them better up close."

Dave took the net from Chris. "Here, I've got a better angle where I am if you were to bring the boat a tad closer."

Chris started the boat and inched it closer, until Dave was within reach.

"I got some!" Dave bellowed as he scooped up a few bottles in the net and brought the dripping objects inside.

Everyone on the deck now piled inside to get a better look.

Ted picked up a bottle to examine it closer. "Well, wherever these were, they were preserved pretty well. They definitely look like antiques. They may be valuable."

Chris inspected a bottle, then set it down. "Well, I'm sure they may be even more valuable to Cape May's Historical Society. I'll make some calls."

Albert coughed. "Are you sure about this? They could be worth a lot of money."

Out on the deck, a scream could be heard as Susan leaned over the railing and dropped her binoculars overboard.

Chris pointed. "Well, those *binoculars* that your wife just dropped into the water are worth a lot of money. Grab a net."

Albert searched the water for the binoculars with a net while everyone else passed around and felt the smooth texture of the bottles. They were in all sizes and all colors, and looked to be very old—maybe even centuries old.

Margaret's bottle was corked with a piece of paper in it. She stood off to the side trying to pull the note out, but the mouth of the bottle was too thin. She grabbed a pen out of her purse and finally jimmied the note out carefully.

Dearest John,

If you find this, I'm out to sea with my father. The boat has started taking on water, and I fear the worst. If our marriage is to never come, know that I love you.

Alexandra

Margaret's heart dropped as she read the note over and over, not believing what she was seeing or if it was even real. It had to be authentic. The writing was an old-style cursive, the paper was aged, the bottle was vintage, and it was all unearthed after a hurricane. It had to be.

Margaret was jolted out of her thoughts by a loud, excited scream.

"We got the binoculars! We got them!" Susan happily yelled as she held them up for everyone on the boat to see.

CHAPTER TEN

Sarah smoothed her skirt and patiently waited for Christine and the gardening club to arrive at the Monarch Coffeehouse. She'd set chairs up facing the big windows at the front of the building, framing a nice, if somewhat cloudy, autumn view. She glanced at Dawn and her other employees who were busy helping customers and making drinks, and felt a sense of relief. It was good to know her coffeehouse was in capable hands.

The front door swung open as Christine plowed inside looking disheveled. "It sure looks like it's going to rain out there," she said while looking over her shoulder out the door.

Sarah crinkled her brow and walked over to the front door, opening it wide, when a humid but slightly chilly mist caused her to shiver with a chill. "Well, that's odd. I hadn't read anything of the sort in the weather today."

Just as she was about to shut the door, the Pittsburgh visitors, along with Margaret and Liz, started walking up the street towards the coffeehouse.

"Welcome, everyone!" Sarah said, forcing a chipper smile though it was early in the morning.

Margaret and Liz stopped to give Sarah a hug. "We can't thank you enough for doing this," Liz said.

Everyone piled in, browsing around a little to look at all of the displays of books and mugs, before finally taking their seats.

Sarah stood facing everyone. "Hello! I'm Sarah, a friend of Margaret and Liz's. This is my coffeehouse and it's appropriately named the Monarch Coffeehouse after the monarch butterflies, which I hear you are here in Cape May to see."

Everyone smiled and nodded.

"That's right!" Marcy rambunctiously yelled from the back.

Sarah chuckled. "Well, we've concocted a monarch butterfly coffee drink for those who'd like to try a fun, themed drink, and of course we also have all of the normal coffee drinks, as well. If you'd like, grab something now before we start the presentation."

After the group got their coffees and sat back down, Christine stood at the front with her laptop on a table and some papers with lots of notes reciting what she was going to say.

Sarah put her hand on Christine's shoulder. "You got this?"

Christine turned to look at Sarah and sweat all but poured down her face. "Uh ... I think so? I'm a little nervous. I don't remember the last time I gave a presentation like this."

Just as Sarah was about to offer a pep talk to Christine, she bolted for the bathroom. "If I don't make it back out, you can use my notes," Christine said as she slammed and locked the door.

Sarah looked at Margaret with widened eyes, then grabbed Christine's notes. "Well, I guess I'll begin." Addressing her audience, she said, "Did you know the monarch butterfly travels over two thousand miles during migration along the Atlantic coast to Mexico? Between September and October is when they usually make a pit stop in Cape May during their journey."

A customer's surprised shout as they dropped their hot coffee cup disrupted Sarah and turned everyone's attention to the other side of the room.

Sarah looked around the coffeehouse, now sweating like Christine had been. "Anyway, as I was saying …The monarch population has greatly declined over the years due to a decrease in milkweed. Milkweed is the monarch caterpillar's only source of food, and everyone is encouraged to plant it in their yards."

Interrupted by a loud crack of thunder, Sarah noted the skies had gone from gray to black. The sounds of rain lightly pitter-pattering on the roof could be heard all throughout the shop. Sarah took a deep breath, composing herself again, when Judy and Bob walked through the front door, holding their jackets over their heads.

"Did we miss anything? We were running late. The skies just opened up on us," Judy said as she found a seat next to Joyce and Brian.

Margaret and Liz looked over at Judy and Bob, chuckling and shaking their heads while Sarah grabbed a napkin from her purse and blotted the sweat from her forehead. She looked at the bathroom door that was still closed with Christine in it. *Christine. Get out here please*, Sarah thought to herself.

The front door opened again, this time another couple barreled in out of the rain. Sarah stared, adjusting her eyes to make sure she was seeing correctly. Chris's parents were the last people on earth she wanted to see right now. Why had they come to her coffeehouse after that awkward situation during the hurricane?

Instead of heading to the coffee counter, Chris's parents walked right over to the presentation and took a seat in the back. Sarah froze like a deer in headlights. Sweat now poured off of her like a faucet, and she was about to pull a Christine and make a run for it.

Margaret and Liz, having no clue who Chris's parents were, stared at Sarah and mouthed, "Are you OK?" to her.

Sarah shook her head. "You want to take over? I've got

something to handle," Sarah said before booking it to the employee area in the back.

Margaret got up with her coffee in hand, set it down, and looked at the Monarch notes. It was pages and pages long. She stared at it as all of the B&B guests stared back at her, then tossed the notes on the table.

"OK, everyone. Change of plans. I know it's raining, but I think it's going to stop soon, so we're going to head to the Cape May Meadows and Garrett Family Preserve to observe the butterflies. What do you think?"

The group looked around at each other and nodded, then got up from their chairs.

Margaret and Liz walked to the back employee area to find Sarah sitting on a chair taking deep breaths.

"What's going on?" Margaret asked, concerned.

Sarah rubbed her temples. "Uh, everything. First of all, I wasn't prepared to give Christine's presentation. Second of all, I kept getting disrupted and distracted while reading her notes. Third of all, Chris's parents are that couple that joined the group last."

Liz poked her head back into the room. "Are you serious? Why's that an issue?"

Margaret sighed. "I guess I forgot to tell you. She stayed at the B&B during the hurricane to … get away from them."

Sarah nodded. "Yes, I did. It was the most awkward, awful experience. Chris and I had a fight over it. I put myself in danger fleeing their house."

Liz nodded. "Yikes. Well, they're still sitting out there. Maybe you should go talk to them. We're going to take everyone to the Meadows and the Preserve."

Sarah reached over and grabbed both of their wrists. "Please. Don't leave me alone with them. Can you come over with me?"

Margaret shifted her eyes. "Well, then *we're* going to feel really awkward."

Sarah pulled her phone out of her pocket and called Chris, then set the phone down. "Straight to voice mail. He's on the boat. Ugh!"

Liz poked her head out again. "Look, they're just sitting there like they're waiting for you. Go talk to them."

Sarah nodded, took a hard gulp, and stood up, making sure to smooth her skirt again. "OK, I'm going to do it. I'll talk to you guys later. So sorry this didn't go as planned."

Margaret flicked her hand in the air. "Don't worry about it. The group seemed to enjoy the coffees and getting to see the place. Let us know how it goes."

Sarah walked slowly back out to the chairs, which Chris's parents now were the only ones in them. "Oh, hi there. What are you two doing here?"

Cynthia stood up immediately. "Hi, Sarah. We were coming to join the monarch butterfly presentation that Chris told us about. It looks like we got here too late, though," she said as she glanced around at the empty chairs.

Charles laughed. "That's our Chris, always giving us the wrong time."

Sarah sighed. "Well, my presenter got cold feet, leaving me to do the presentation, and let's just say that didn't go well. The group just left for a tour around Cape May to see the butterflies, so the presentation is over ... or never happened in the first place, really."

Cynthia stared at Sarah, almost like she was trying to analyze her. "Well, to be honest, we aren't really interested in monarch butterflies. We just wanted to come and apologize for what happened the other night. We were out of line ... and we're sorry."

Charles looked the other way and Cynthia nudged him hard. "Yes, that's right. We're both sorry. Won't you come back for dinner? We'll do it right this time," Charles said.

Sarah took a deep, relieved breath on the inside. Maybe they weren't as bad as she thought they were. "Well, actually,

Chris and I were thinking it'd be nice for you two to come our place for dinner. What do you say?"

Cynthia face brightened. "We'd like that."

* * *

The skies cleared up just in time for their venture around Cape May Meadows. Luckily, Bonnie and Irene were able to come back to the coffeehouse earlier than planned to pick up the rest of the group.

The goldenrod on either side of the walking trail had the bright orange-and-black monarchs scattered throughout, causing the group to hurry over, while Margaret and Liz trailed in the back.

"So, I found something when we were out on Chris's boat the other day," Margaret said with a slight smirk.

Liz cocked her head. "What?"

Margaret pulled the little bottle of out of her purse and handed it to Liz.

Liz examined the bottle. "An old bottle? OK, that's cool," Liz said as she handed it back to Margaret.

Margaret sighed and handed it back to her. "Look inside of it."

Liz squinted her eyes and looked inside the bottle, noticing the small rolled piece of paper, then quickly pulled it out to look at it. "It's a love note. Wow."

Margaret nodded. "A very old love note from what I can tell. We found a lot of these bottles on the boat with Chris, and he handed them over to the Cape May Historical Society. I kind of hid this one and held onto it."

Liz rolled the piece of paper up and stuck it back into the bottle, then handed it back. "Well, this is pretty special. What are you going to do with it?"

Margaret rubbed her fingers over the bright-blue glass, almost as if trying to feel the answer. "I'm not sure yet. It was too romantic to let go. Maybe I'll turn it in eventually. I just feel some sort of pull to it. I'm guessing this couple never got back together. It sounded like the boat maybe capsized or sank, and this was her one last attempt at contacting the love of her life."

Liz looked over at their guests huddled around the butterflies. "Well maybe, but you don't know that. Maybe they got rescued, but the bottles didn't, and she went off and married her dearest John."

"I sure hope so," Margaret said as she stared down at the beautiful engagement ring that Dave gave her.

Liz took notice. "Speaking of marriage. How's the wedding planning go?"

Margaret looked up from her ring and shrugged her shoulders. "Nothing's planned. We had both expected to have everything figured out by now, but between being unprepared for this Pittsburgh group, finding new hires for the B&B, and the hurricane, it's all been put on the back burner. It's looking like it probably won't happen this fall," Margaret said with a sigh.

Liz made a sad face. "I know you two wanted to get married rather quickly. Maybe waiting will make it that much more exciting."

Margaret held the blue bottle up to the light and stared at it. "I'm feeling a little like Alexandra at the moment. I want to marry Dave before the boat I'm on capsizes and it's too late. I'm already forty-six years old. I've spent my whole life waiting for someone like Dave to sweep me off my feet. He's everything I've ever wanted, and I don't want to wait."

Liz smiled, while looking at the most in love she'd ever seen her sister. "Well, have you told him that? That you don't want to wait?"

Margaret paused in thought. "Not exactly. I went with my brain instead of my heart and told him we need to wait until next year so we can do it right. I'm starting to rethink that ...."

Liz put her hand on Margaret's shoulder as her phone rang.

"Hello? Oh, hi, Lilly! Is everything OK with the design?"

Lilly laughed. "Oh, everything is perfectly fine. You do amazing work. I did have some important information for you, though. You'd mentioned finding things to do for your B&B guests who were interested in monarch butterflies. A friend of mine is opening a little gallery today all centered around butterfly paintings. I hear there are plenty of monarch butterfly ones there. I'll send you the address."

Liz thanked her client and hung up the phone, then glanced back at Margaret, who stood staring at her. "Looks like we have a gallery to attend in Cape May."

* * *

Dale manned his funnel cake stand at the high school football game where he was set up for the day. His employee was frying up some funnel cakes in the sizzling oil when he decided to step out of the cart and get some fresh air. He walked over to the chain-link fence that surrounded the field and leaned on it, watching a great tackle happen from the home team.

"Dale?"

Dale turned around to see a man standing behind him, clad in a swanky business suit and shoes.

"Yeah?" Dale asked.

"Do you remember me from the softball game?"

Dale crossed his arms and squinted his eyes. "I'm drawing a blank. Fill me in."

"I was at the softball game. Donna's …"

Dale's heart sank as he immediately remembered. "Are you Adam? Donna's ex?"

Adam nodded. "Yeah. I guess I look a little different dressed like this. I have a client to meet in thirty minutes before I board my plane back to California."

Dale nodded, not sure of what to say next.

Adam looked out onto the field. "That's my nephew on the away team. My sister told me about the game, and I thought it was best to stop by, and I happened to see you over here. I guess I wanted to talk about Donna."

Dale's stomach flipped as he quickly glanced at the food cart to make eye contact with his employee, who nodded back at him. "OK, I guess we can do that."

Adam kicked a rock next to his shoe. "So, you two are dating, right?"

Dale looked back at Adam. "Look, Adam. I know you two are divorced. I'm divorced as well. I've been there. It isn't easy, I know that—"

Adam cut in. "I just need to know. Are you two happy?"

Dale's eyes widened. He didn't know how to answer this question. They had broken up not too long ago, and had just started fresh over. He was happy for sure, but was Donna?

Adam looked over to the football field, watching his nephew's team score a touchdown before looking back to Dale. "Look, I just need to know that she's happy and there isn't a chance of us getting back together. Then I can move on."

Dale glanced back at his employee, who was now waving him over. "Look, Adam. My employee needs me back at the cart, but I'll say this. I can't speak for Donna, but I'm happy, and I'd like to think that she is too. We've only been together a few months, and even if we weren't happy, it doesn't necessarily mean that she'd want to get back with you, you know? It's probably time to move on. Find yourself someone else who makes you happy."

Adam sighed. "Yeah, I tried that. It didn't work out. She couldn't compare to Donna. It's all my fault that our marriage didn't work. I guess I'll have to live with it."

Dale's eyes softened, and he put his hand on Adam's shoulder. "You will be happy again, Adam. Trust me. I was once in your shoes. Give it time."

Adam started back towards the visitors' bleachers on the other side of the field, then he turned back around. "Just do me a favor. Treat her right. Don't ruin a good thing like I did. She loves Cape May. Don't pull her away from it."

Dale nodded. "Luckily, I'm just as in love with Cape May as she is."

CHAPTER ELEVEN

Bright and early the next morning, everyone gathered on the wood deck platform at Cape May Point State Park to look for the migrating hawks. It wasn't exactly monarch butterflies, but the Pittsburgh visitors were excited to go birding. Sarah joined in and stood next to Chris as he gave his speech to the group about what to look for with the binoculars.

Another large group of birders stood with their vented button-down shirts, pants, and hats. They were pretty easy to spot out of a crowd. They quietly talked amongst each other, some aiming their huge long-focus lens at the landscape while others peered through binoculars.

Sharon and Ted stood amongst the group, holding Dipsey and Doodle in their carrier bag (since having learned their lesson at Liz and Greg's), and loudly gasped at every hawk that flew overhead and across the pond before them.

"Did you see that one, hon?" Sharon asked.

Ted held his binoculars aloft and searched the sky. "I see him. There he is!"

Sharon turned to a lady next to her from the other birding group and tapped her on the shoulder. "This is amazing, isn't it?"

The lady nodded, then looked back up at a passing hawk. "It sure is. We travel across the country every year to see them."

Sharon smiled. "Well, we came as far as Pittsburgh."

Another member in the lady's group chimed in. "We're from Ohio. Cape May has some of the best hawk watching in the world."

Margaret and Liz stood off to the side when a peregrine falcon flew across the trees right past them. They wondered how they'd lived in Cape May this long and had never come out to watch the hawk migration when people flew in from across the country just to watch them.

On the other side of the deck, Chris put his arm around Sarah as they gazed up at the sky together, admiring the beautiful birds of prey. Chris paused for a moment in thought. "Whatever happened with the bad review of your coffeehouse that woman tried to stop from going to press?"

Sarah laughed. "Oh, Christine? She actually got ahold of me and apologized about running out on her monarch presentation. I thought it was cold feet, but she thinks she had food poisoning. Luckily, her editor pulled the review and Christine submitted a new one. I'll have to keep my eye out for it."

Chris sighed. "Well, that's a relief. I'm glad it all worked out in the end."

Sarah nodded and pulled him in even closer. "So, now that everything is smoothed over with your parents, should we have them over for dinner to start over?"

Chris looked back at Sarah with widened eyes. "Really? You think you're ready?"

Sarah smiled while gazing up at the sky. "Well, I think it's important that I'm on good terms with the parents of the man I love."

Chris leaned down to kiss Sarah but was interrupted by a scream.

"My dogs! Get back here, Dipsey and Doodle!" Sharon

yelled out as her Yorkies found an unzipped part of the carrier and made a run for it off the platform, towards the pond right underneath where all of the hawks were flying. The other birding group gasped as they watched two little hawk meals out on the loose.

As Sharon and Ted made a beeline for the dogs, Marcy slapped her forehead. "I told them not to bring the dogs. This is not the place for them. Have they not learned anything from what happened on the farm?"

Joyce shook her head. "They insisted that they'd be fine in the carrier, but that didn't turn out to be so."

Everyone watched as Sharon and Ted got closer to Dipsey and Doodle, when suddenly Sharon rolled her ankle and took a tumble on the sandy dirt trail they were running on. Ted looked after the dogs, who were getting away, then back at Sharon, and ultimately went back to help Sharon, who screamed out in pain.

Chris shook his head and, without a second thought, hopped the rail of the deck. Speeding past Sharon and Ted, he scooped the Yorkies up one by one just as a hawk dove down towards them with his talons out, ready to scoop them up. He unbuttoned his flannel and stuffed them inside for safety.

Ted helped Sharon up, supporting her weight as she hobbled on her good ankle towards Chris. "My babies. Mommy loves you so."

Chris wiped the sweat from his brow. "I'd hand them over, but I really think we need to get them into their carrier. This isn't the place for them. They could have easily been a hawk snack. You're lucky. They're lucky."

Margaret and Liz cleared a bench for Sharon, who was happy to sit down and examine her ankle, which was now the size of a softball.

"How about we take you back so you can ice your ankle?" Margaret asked as she watched Sharon writhe in pain.

Sharon shakily stood up, limping slowly on her ankle. "I'm fine. It's swollen, but I don't want to miss the gallery."

Ted sighed. "Hon, we really should go back."

Sharon shook her head. "No. I didn't come all the way out here to sit at the B&B. I'll be fine. I'm going to go hang out in the car with the dogs. You all take your time."

Chris walked back up onto the deck and leaned against the rail next to Sarah, his tanned arms from being out on the water everyday glistening in the sun. "Well, I think that was the most heroic thing I've ever seen with my own eyes," Sarah casually said with a chuckle, trying to keep her adoration subtle.

Chris ran his hands through his hair and laughed. "Yeah, it was something."

Sarah inched closer to Chris and grabbed his hand. "My very own hero. I'm glad to call you mine."

* * *

About an hour later, they pulled up to the little art gallery in town that Liz's client invited them to. Liz stepped out of her car and stood next to Margaret as the B&B guests funneled inside the quaint little place.

"This place is adorable, Liz. I'm going to have to come back another time," Margaret said as she looked through the window.

Liz sighed. "I'm pretty sure this is just a pop-up thing for the monarch butterflies. I don't think they showcase paintings year-round."

Margaret bit her lip. "Well, let's go in and—" She stopped abruptly at the sound of their names being called from down the street.

"Am I crazy or did Mom call our names?" Liz asked.

Margaret laughed. "If you're crazy, then I'm crazy, because I heard it too."

Judy and Bob walked right up to them, waving their hands.

"Hey, you two! What are you up to?" Judy asked.

"We're about to check out this little pop-up art gallery with the group. Would you two like to join us?" Margaret asked.

Judy looked through the window. "Well, I think we could come in a for a minute. Why not?"

Bob shrugged. "Sounds good to me."

Once they got inside, jazz music played over the speakers, and everyone held glasses of wine in hand as they studied and talked about each painting.

A woman dressed in all black came up to them. "Hello, I'm Norma. Welcome to the art show. Would you care for a glass of wine?"

Sarah looked at her watch. "It's not even lunchtime yet. I don't know …"

Judy nodded enthusiastically. "Heck yeah. Wine and paintings go perfect together, no?"

Bob rolled his eyes. "Do you have coffee?"

Norma pointed to the table off to the side. "We actually do, over there. Help yourself to a cup."

Margaret and Liz followed Judy over to the wine table, where plenty of wine bottles from local wineries sat.

Margaret poured three wine glasses and handed one to Judy and Liz. "You only live once? Right?"

Liz toasted with her sister and mother, gently clinking glasses together, before taking a sip. "Correct, but we have to drive. So, this is our first and last."

The three of them maneuvered their way through the gallery, taking time to talk to their Pittsburgh guests here and there.

Liz stood before a large watercolor painting that looked magical. The monarch butterflies had some sort of metallic sheen that made them sparkle and glow under the lights in the gallery.

"Mom, Margaret, come look at this painting. It's stunning," Liz said as she took the last sip of her wine.

Judy and Margaret stood next to Liz, admiring the work, when Norma appeared next to them.

"It's great, isn't it? My husband painted this one. Are you all monarch butterfly enthusiasts?" Norma asked.

Before they could answer, Marcy overheard and walked over. "We definitely are. Our Pittsburgh gardening club came all the way here and rode out a hurricane just to see them."

Norma nodded in thought. "How about this. Have you all finished looking around the gallery? If so, my husband and I live a couple blocks away. If you'd like to see our elaborate butterfly garden, I'd be happy to show you. We actually try to rescue the monarch butterflies ourselves. Do you know that in the wild, monarch butterflies only have around a five percent chance of making it from egg to butterfly? My husband and I find the eggs and let them hatch protected indoors, then we release them. I'll have my coworker stay at the gallery while we walk over."

Marcy and Joyce did a little clap of excitement. "We can't wait. Can we bring the wine?"

Norma laughed. "Well, you may have to leave that here."

Everyone filed out of the little art gallery and followed Norma down the street to her gorgeous bright-green Victorian.

Norma opened the pink wrought iron gate to her front yard, while everyone followed behind. The yard was full of milkweed, sunflowers, butterfly bushes, goldenrod, and other gorgeous plants to attract and help the butterflies thrive. A man stood in the yard examining something under a magnifying glass, completely unaware that a group of people had just entered his yard.

"Bert, we have visitors," Norma said while nodding towards the group.

Bert stopped what he was doing, turned around and smiled. "Well, that's a surprise. What brings you all here?"

Norma pointed to a cluster of butterflies on their flowers. "They are here to see the monarch butterflies. Came all the way from Pittsburgh. They were at the gallery, and I just had to show them our butterfly garden. We see so many monarchs here."

Bert set down his magnifying glass. "Come on inside, and I'll show you some newly hatched monarchs that we're getting ready to release today, actually."

Ecstatic to see this side of monarch butterfly conservation, the garden club followed Bert and Norma inside, where there was both emerged butterflies and some still in the chrysalis stage.

Margaret looked around the room as Bert lectured good-naturedly, and turned to Liz. "Where's Mom and Dad?"

Liz scanned the room. "Did they stay behind at the art gallery?"

Margaret shook her head. "No, I'm pretty sure they came with us."

Liz and Margaret stepped out of the house and back into the butterfly garden to look for their parents.

"There they are," Liz said after she saw them sitting on a bench amongst the flowers and butterflies.

Margaret glanced across the yard to see both Bob and Judy pouring wine out of the wine bottle, sharing a peaceful moment amongst the graceful butterflies.

Liz shook her head. "They totally swiped that wine bottle from the art gallery and brought it here."

Margaret laughed. "They sure did, but look at 'em. They look so happy. I can't blame them."

Liz smiled, then looked at her watch. "I have to get to Heirloom to prepare for tonight."

Margaret nodded. "That's right. What time should we arrive?"

"I think five thirty is what Greg planned. I'm pretty excited," Liz said as she started walking back towards the gate.

* * *

Greg reserved the outdoor backyard space of his restaurant, Heirloom, for the gardening club as part of the effort to help Margaret and Liz.

Liz helped decorate the seating area by adding purple potted mums on the tables with clip-on monarch butterflies. The tablecloths were orange, and each place setting had a small package of milkweed seeds with planting instructions.

Greg walked around the tables, placing the small butterfly-themed menu on each plate. "Well, I hope they like what I've prepared. I've never done a special menu like this before, but I'm pretty proud of what the chefs came up with."

Before Liz could say anything, the Pittsburgh Gardening Club arrived, spilling into the backyard as they each began claiming their seats.

Sharon clapped her hands together. "This is exquisite, isn't it, hon?" she asked Ted.

Ted nodded while taking a sip of ice water and reading over the bill of fare. "It is, dear."

Marcy glanced at the curated menu. While the dishes didn't exactly portray the monarch butterfly, they had a lot of the vibrant orange colors throughout.

When Dale walked outside holding a microphone stand and guitar, Liz furrowed her brow. He sat down on a chair on the other side of the outdoor area and Greg nodded to him.

"You didn't tell me Dale was coming," Liz said to her husband. "Is he going to play music out here?"

Greg smiled. "He sure is. He wanted to play a part in helping somehow."

Liz adjusted the tablecloth, then looked back at Dale before picking up her phone, snapping a photo of him, and sending it to Donna with a text. *Look who just arrived. I had no idea he was coming to play. How nice! Did you know?*

Donna immediately texted back. *I didn't know either! Maybe it was a spur-of-the-moment decision? He looks cute with that guitar.*

Liz thought for a moment before responding. *I think you*

should show up with your guitar and surprise him.

Liz waited for a response, but Donna didn't reply, so she stuck her phone back in her pocket.

Dale played his guitar while everyone put their orders in and opened up bottles of wine.

Margaret helped Greg and Liz bring the food and drinks out but paused once in a while to take a breather. It had been a whirlwind two weeks, and tomorrow was the group's last day at the inn. She could only hope that they'd had a good time.

Once everyone had received their meals, Donna walked in off the street holding her guitar case. She glanced around the yard until her eyes locked on Dale's in the corner. He was mid-song and kept playing, but a wide smile spread across his face.

Liz quickly put a chair next to Dale, and Donna sat, pulling her guitar out while smiling at Dale as he finished the song. Without saying a word, and with their eyes locked on each other, they both smiled and began to strum the first notes of the next song. By some unspoken language, they instinctively knew what the other was playing.

Donna laughed as she played, feeling herself blush and warm with emotion.

Dale nodded at her while still strumming. "Hey, you."

Donna smiled while taking over the lead of the song and nodded back at him. "Hi, there. Guess what?"

Dale's eyes widened.

Donna glanced around the yard while strumming, then back at Dale. "Adam told me what happened yesterday."

Dale gulped hard. "I should have been the one to tell you we talked, not him."

Donna smiled. "It's OK. I'm just letting you know that I *am* happy … with you, in case you were wondering."

Dale stood up abruptly with guitar in hand, performing an impromptu solo before finishing the song a minute later and sitting back down. "I'm really glad to hear that because so am I."

CHAPTER TWELVE

It was the B&B guests last full day in Cape May, and they were surely going out with a bang as the Monarch Butterfly Festival and Lima Bean Festival were happening on the same day due to the hurricane causing delays.

Margaret, though completely exhausted from working every day at the Seahorse and every night for her job at the wildlife refuge, managed to wake herself up early to walk with the group to the Monarch Festival. Once they arrived, Margaret spotted Gina waving enthusiastically from her tent.

"Hey, everyone! Are you ready to hand out lots of milk-weed seeds and monarch butterfly pamphlets today?" Gina asked excitedly.

They all happily grabbed bags full of the milkweed seeds and bundles of packets, and found their spots to stand, while a few others convened inside the tent to help get Gina's photography prints of the butterflies organized for buyers.

Gina glanced at Margaret as she yawned. "How are you holding up?"

Margaret gave a half smile. "Well, the last two weeks have been a whirlwind. I've practically been working two full-time jobs. I'm excited for things to go back to normal, especially when Dolly and Kim come back to the Seahorse from their extended break."

Liz suddenly appeared next to them. "Hey. Sorry, I had an errand to run, and it went later than expected. What did I miss?"

Margaret rubbed her eyes. "Oh, just the fact that I need coffee stat, and that I'm very much looking forward to Dolly and Kim coming back. Irene, Jackie, and Bonnie have done an outstanding job, but I've realized these past two weeks that I've worked myself to the bone."

Liz put her arm around Margaret. "You've gotten stuck at the Seahorse more than I have, especially with that hurricane, and I apologize. I know it must have been hard for you to balance everything. When are Dolly and Kim coming back?"

Margaret shrugged. "I'm not exactly sure. I don't think until November."

Liz glanced at Gina and winked. "Hey, how about you and I go walk around the festival and get some coffee. Let's enjoy ourselves. Gina and our guests are all set."

"Sounds good, sister," Margaret said as they started walking towards the long stretch of tents featuring a variety of vendors.

They stopped at the Monarch Coffeehouse tent, where Sarah and Chris stood with full aprons on.

"Hey, you two!" Sarah said surprised.

Margaret laughed. "Hey, I didn't know you were going to be here … with Chris to boot. Hey, Chris!"

Liz chimed in. "It's our Pittsburgh guests' last day, and they're with Gina, who has them handing out seeds and butterfly pamphlets. They'll walk around in a bit, I'm sure, but they seem to enjoy helping out."

Sarah put her arm around Chris. "Well, you know me and my last-minute shenanigans. I somehow was able to secure a booth, and Chris offered to help. It's the first time he's worked with me, and I'm kind of loving it," Sarah said as she glanced up at Chris with a smile.

Chris nodded. "It's nice little change from being on the boat. What would you two like to drink?"

"I'll have a light roast coffee. What about you, Liz?" Margaret asked.

"Same for me," Liz said as she glanced around the festival that had started to get crowded.

Sarah poured the coffees while Chris snapped the lids on top and handed them their hot drinks. "It's on the house, of course," Sarah said joyfully.

"Oh, you don't have to do that. We'll gladly pay," Margaret said pushing cash towards Sarah's waving hand.

"Nope. Keep your money. I don't want it. I need all of the good karma I can get. Tonight, we're having Chris's parents over for the first time after that debacle during the hurricane," Sarah said while nudging Chris.

Liz paused for a moment in thought. "Oh, that's right. I forgot they showed up at the Monarch Coffeehouse afterwards. Did everything go well then?"

"Yes, I think so. I'm glad to finally be doing this," Sarah said glancing up at Chris with a smile.

Chris put his arm around Sarah again then looked down at her with an expression of complete adoration. "Frankly, I couldn't be happier that you're even trying after what happened."

Noticing a lot of people had formed a line behind her and Liz to get coffee, Margaret said, "Well, we'll leave you two at it. Good luck with the coffee tent today."

As the sisters strolled away, a group of school-aged children walked by wearing monarch butterfly wings while fluttering their arms up and down to showcase that they were butterflies.

"Liz, look at how adorable they look," Margaret said, smiling at the children.

Liz chuckled. "Take a closer look, Margaret. I think your daughters are in there."

Margaret gasped. "Harper! Abby! Over here!"

"Hi, Mom! Hi, Aunt Liz!" Harper and Abby yelled as they waved from the little walking parade they were in.

Margaret looked around the festival. "I guess Mom and Dad brought them here?"

"Must have, but that means my boys are here too. Oh, look —there's Mom following behind the kids way in the back."

"Mom!" Margaret yelled through the crowd.

Judy walked up with a smile on her face. "Well, we thought we'd bring the kids to the festival. They love it. Did you see the girls' pretty butterflies painted on their faces?"

Margaret smiled as she and Liz walked with Judy behind the kid parade. "I did. They look adorable and happy."

Liz cut in. "Where are Steven and Michael and Dad? Back home?"

Judy laughed. "You won't believe where they are," she said as she pointed to a large grassy area up ahead.

Margaret and Liz squinted their eyes to get a better look, noticing many people sitting on yoga matts stretching.

Liz laughed. "Dad and the boys are doing yoga over there? Am I seeing this correctly?"

Judy nodded. "The boys said they wanted to do it, and asked Bob to go. He couldn't tell them no. I'm getting a kick out of it myself. Never thought I'd see my husband do yoga."

Margaret and Liz chuckled as they glanced over and saw their dad unsteadily attempt the tree pose before almost tumbling over onto Steven and Michael's mats that were set up next to his.

Judy watched the parade of children with Harper and Abby starting to move more quickly through the crowd. "I've got to catch up to the girls. You two go on and enjoy the festival."

Margaret and Liz said their goodbyes, and immediately

caught the eye of Sharon and Ted who had positioned themselves farther away from Gina's tent, handing out seeds and pamphlets.

"How's it going out here? Lots of takers with the seeds?" Liz asked the couple.

Ted smiled with his big camera hung around his neck, per usual. "Oh, plenty. We've had people come back and ask if they can have more for their friends. I'm feeling good about handing these out. I hope it will really help out the monarch population."

Sharon, who had Dipsey and Doodle on leashes, nodded in agreement. "I have to say. I love being out here. It feels like we're making a change by doing this, as small as it is."

Margaret bent down to pet Dipsey and Doodle as the little Yorkies panted happily by Sharon's legs. "Well, these little guys sure got an experience out of these past two weeks. I'm glad they made it through."

Ted laughed. "Same, here. We're leaving them with Sharon's mother next time."

Sharon glanced at a woman walking by with chili. "Oh, I could really go for some food. Where is that from?"

The woman smiled. "The Lima Bean Festival. It's a few blocks that way. They have the most delicious lima bean chili. It's a must try."

Sharon's eyes widened. "Thank you."

When the rest of the gardening club walked up behind them, Susan said, "Well, we're plumb out of the seed packets and pamphlets. What's everyone up to?"

Sharon pointed to the woman that had the soup. "Well, there's the Lima Bean Festival a few blocks that way. Anyone want to go with us to grab something to eat? We can come back and walk around afterwards."

The group nodded affirmatively before following Dipsey and Doodle, who led the way ahead of Sharon and Ted while Margaret and Liz happily trailed along behind the group, bringing up the rear. They arrived to find a lot more tents, but this time with tons of fresh green lima beans to purchase.

Marcy walked over to a stand selling lima bean shirts and sweatshirts. She held one up to her and looked at the group. "What do you think?" Everyone nodded their approval before swarming the booth and purchasing a Lima Bean Festival T-shirt or hat for themselves.

Dipsey and Doodle pulled Sharon towards a homemade dog treat vendor where some were made to look like green lima beans, while everyone else searched out the famous lima bean chili.

"The lima bean chili is over here, guys!" Liz said as she stood in line behind a few others waiting to get in on the delicious-smelling food.

Margaret laughed. "I'm not sure they heard you. They're eyeing the pottery."

Liz shrugged. "Well, more for you and me, then."

From behind them, Gina said, "Hey, you two! Getting that yummy chili, I see. I'm getting some myself."

Margaret put her hand on Gina's shoulder. "Glad to see you taking a break. Did you get someone to watch the tent?"

Gina laughed. "Nope. I'm sold out of what I brought. I packed the car up already. Just have to take down the tent and I'm set."

Liz smiled. "You're kidding! Wow, what a success!"

Gina looked at her watch. "You're telling me. Anyway, I'm going to head over to see the monarch butterflies in Cape May Point. There're thousands of them perched on the pines according to some friends of mine. Want to bring the group along for one last sighting before they leave tomorrow?"

The Pittsburgh guests joined them in line as Margaret was about to answer. "Well, I guess we can ask them now. Hey, everyone! There's been thousands of monarchs sighted in Cape May Point. Want to get some chili and we'll head over with Gina?"

Dipsey and Doodle barked at some passing dogs just as Marcy said, "Yes! My goodness, yes!" and bent down to pet and calm the Yorkies.

Ted was the last to walk over, and he sported a bright-green lima bean hat and oversized lima bean shirt. "What did I miss?"

Sharon laughed. "You stick out like a sore thumb, hon. We're about to go see thousands of monarchs after we grab some chili. Get your camera ready."

* * *

By early evening, Liz and Margaret had managed to get everyone over to Cape May Point, including Judy and Bob who brought their grandkids. Gina met them by the sandy dunes, but there wasn't another soul around for as far as the eye could see.

Gina smiled. "This is my secret spot. Not many people know about it except for some friends in my inner circle. They told me that up the beach trail to the dunes is where we will find them. Let's cross our fingers they're still there."

When a truck pulled up along the beach street, everyone glanced over to see who it was. Margaret's heart leaped at the sight of her handsome man dressed in a gray T-shirt that was just tight enough to subtly showcase his strong arms.

"Hey, you," Dave said as he walked around the front of his truck to join them. He placed his hand on the small of Margaret's back, eyes only for her, not even paying attention to anyone else around.

Margaret leaned her head into his side as he pulled her in close. "How did you know where to find us?"

Dave smiled. "Greg told me. He hoped to get over here too, but got stuck at the restaurant. So I figured I'd go for the both of us."

Gina cleared her throat. "OK, we ready to head up? I'm assuming we have everyone now?"

Sharon smiled. "We sure are ready!"

"Great, follow me," Gina said as she walked up the sandy beach trail.

At the top where the dunes were, over five thousand monarchs sat roosting in huge clusters—a virtual sea of bright orange and black.

Everyone stood in silence, especially Sharon and Ted, who had dropped the Yorkies off at the Seahorse prior. There was nothing to be said in that moment. Everyone just watched the magnificent beauty of nature before them.

After an hour or so of snapping photographs and taking in the special moment that they had traveled so far for and withstood a hurricane to see, Ted looked over at the group.

"We haven't gotten a group photo yet, and today is our last day. How about it?" Ted asked holding his camera.

Margaret walked to Ted. "I can take the photo so you can be in it. Why don't you all stand right here so we can see the butterflies in the background?"

The group huddled tightly together, all of their arms around each other as Margaret held the fancy camera up to her eye. *Click. Click. Click.*

Everyone started striking up conversation as Ted grabbed his camera back from Margaret and took a look at the photos she took. "Not bad. You really positioned the photo nicely. I'm going to edit this back home to really make the colors pop. Thank you."

Margaret smiled. "Sure thing. How about we give Gina a big thanks for bringing us to this amazing spot."

Everyone said their thank yous and then turned to Margaret and Liz.

"We also really have to thank you and Liz for making this one of the most memorable trips of our lives. Thank you so much for everything you've done," Marcy said as she gave Liz and Margaret a hug. Everyone else followed suit, stepping up to hug Margaret and Liz.

Ted pointed his camera again. "Alright, guys. Let's do one last photo. This time with everyone. That includes you, Margaret, Liz, Judy, Bob, and Dave. Get on in there."

The locals groaned but quickly posed together for one last group shot before heading back down the beach trail towards the cars.

Margaret and Liz stood on the dune together after everyone had gone ahead and looked at each other with a sigh of relief.

"We did it. We pulled it off with the help of family and friends. I can't believe it!" Liz said while putting her arm around Margaret's shoulders.

Margaret nodded, staring up ahead at Dave who lended a hand to those having trouble walking on the sandy trail. "We really did."

EPILOGUE

A few days later, Margaret and Dave worked in the garden together. Dave harvested beets while Margaret toted a huge basket of rainbow carrots that she'd plucked from the ground.

Dave wiped the sweat from his brow and chuckled at Margaret as she hauled the carrots over to the table next to his beets.

"What's so funny?" Margaret asked.

Dave gently wiped dirt on her forehead off. "You've been worked to the bone for two weeks, and your first day off you want to work some more here in the garden. I told you that you could rest, and I'd happily take care of all of this."

Margaret gave a satisfied sigh while looking across the lush garden that had started to be encompassed by leaves changing colors on the tree line. "This is a different kind of work, though. It's not stressful at all."

Dave smiled and handed her an empty basket. "Let's go harvest some peas."

They walked together to the peas and Dave started immediately harvesting the pods, putting them into the basket while Margaret only plucked a pod off the vine and popped the fresh candy-like peas into her mouth. Margaret watched Dave's muscles flex as he reached up high to grab peas on the trellis. His light smell of aftershave warmed Margaret's body while she continued eating the peas and watching Dave harvest the pods up and down the trellis.

Dave stopped what he was doing and smiled. "Hungry?"

Margaret popped another pea in her mouth. "You could say that. I've always preferred to eat these fresh over cooking them. They are too delicious. Here, have some," she said, handing him a bunch of peas.

Dave popped them in his mouth and nodded. "They are perfect."

Margaret ran her hands through her hair, pulling the strands up into a ponytail. "So, I know we keep discussing this and then we get too busy to do anything about it, but what's going on with our wedding?"

Dave gave a long sigh then steadied himself while holding onto the trellis and looked back at Margaret. With one hand, he pulled a small little notebook out of his back pocket. "Well, I've made a list of our potential wedding and reception options …."

Margaret put her hand over her mouth and smiled. "You have? That's adorable, Dave."

Dave blushed. "Anyway, these are my ideas for the wedding. The Seahorse Inn, this here garden, or possibly the beach? If we want to get married this fall, we're going to have to find something that's not going to be booked up. These are the ideas that I have. What do you think?"

Margaret smiled. "So, you want to get married this fall, huh? What happened to our discussion about waiting until next year to do it right?"

Dave turned red while staring at his notebook. "Well, um, I was thinking … I'd like to get married as soon as possible. Frankly, I don't want to wait, and I feel like we won't have to wait if we got married somewhere nontraditional."

Margaret was silent while she glanced around the farm full of life and food.

Dave nervously put his notebook back in his pocket. "Would you prefer we married next spring? You're not saying much."

Margaret smiled while popping another fresh pod of peas into her mouth. "I'm sorry. I'm just really taking in this special moment. I would love to get married this fall. I don't care if it's in the kids' tree house. I really don't. Just as long as I get to be your bride. I guess I didn't know how to say that."

Dave looked relieved when he walked over to Margaret and embraced her in a grateful hug. "Same."

Margaret looked up at Dave as they hugged, his skin glowing from the sun setting off in the distance. They both turned to watch the sunset, arms still around each other.

"What about a date for this wedding?" Dave asked still staring at the horizon.

Margaret took a deep breath as she watched birds flying off into the orange sky. "Honestly, as soon as we can. October and November are some of my favorite months, and that would be the perfect time. However, I've actually got a better idea for where our wedding and reception should take place …."

* * *

Pick up **Book 8** in the Cape May Series, **A Cozy Cape May Autumn,** to follow Margaret, Liz, Greg, Dave, and some new characters as well as old familiar ones.

Follow me on Facebook at **www.facebook.com/Claudia-VanceBooks**

ABOUT THE AUTHOR

Claudia Vance is a writer of women's fiction and clean romance. She writes feel good reads that take you to places you'd like to visit with characters you'd want to get to know.

She lives with her boyfriend and 2 cats in a charming small town in New Jersey, not too far from the beautiful beach town of Cape May. She worked behind the scenes on tv shows and film sets for many years, and she's an avid gardener and nature lover.